"What's wrong?" Eden asked in a tight voice

"You kissed me and you've kissed me before. Why behave as though I committed some terrible crime by returning your kisses?"

Silence stretched between them. Finally Joshua spoke again. "Things are getting out of hand here." He gave her a long hard look as he went on. "Affairs I can handle, but I very much doubt if you could. You're the type of woman who expects marriage after a few romps in the hay, figuratively speaking."

"I can't believe you're saying this to me," she returned, trying to keep her voice steady. "I'm not a child. I know the score. You're making it sound as though I've practically begged on my knees for you to make love to me."

She whirled and raced out of the room, humiliated. He was cruel, heartless. How ~~could she have possibly~~ thought she l~~~~

Rosemary Badger, an Australian author, says she always wanted to write, but only started seriously after she took a creative writing course on how to create books specifically for the romance market. Her novels are usually set in Australia, which she knows so well. The author is married and lives with her husband and children in Queensland.

Books by Rosemary Badger

HARLEQUIN ROMANCE

These books may be available at your local bookseller.

Don't miss any of our special offers. Write to us at the following address for information on our newest releases.

Harlequin Reader Service
901 Fuhrmann Blvd., P.O. Box 1397, Buffalo, NY 14240
Canadian address: P.O. Box 2800, Postal Station A,
5170 Yonge St., Willowdale, Ont. M2N 6J3

Shadows of Eden
Rosemary Badger

Harlequin Books

TORONTO • NEW YORK • LONDON
AMSTERDAM • PARIS • SYDNEY • HAMBURG
STOCKHOLM • ATHENS • TOKYO • MILAN

Original hardcover edition published in 1986
by Mills & Boon Limited

ISBN 0-373-02773-7

Harlequin Romance first edition July 1986

The Badger's Four
Mark, Nikki, Matthew, Rachael
For you with love

Printed in U.S.A.

CHAPTER ONE

'. . . COMIN' around the mountain when she comes, oh, we'll all rush out to meet her when . . .' The song was broken in one agonising scream as the car crashed into the guard rail, plunging several metres down the embankment. Afterwards there was only the sound of the rain and then . . . nothing!

Eden sat up in bed and pressed her fingers against her temples. Her blonde hair clung to her head as damp as the nightie which covered her slender form. From the small bedside table she took a bottle of tablets and swallowed two. Slowly the pain in her head diminished leaving only a dull aching throb. Her grey eyes had a lonely, haunted expression as she got out of bed and looked at herself in the mirror.

When would the nightmares end? Would she ever be free of the sight of the articulated lorry skidding towards them, of the sounds of her family screaming as the car rolled over and over, of the deathly silence which followed? Would she ever be free of the whispering voices in her head telling her . . . she didn't know what.

Her family had died that night. Her parents and twin sisters. It had been the twins' sixteenth birthday and they had been returning home after a night of celebrating. Eden had been critically injured, spending months in hospital before finally being discharged. But at the age of twenty she really had nowhere to go. There was the family home and sooner or later she would return to it but she needed a reprieve. Someplace where she could build herself up and sort out the taunting voices in her head.

It had been Doc McKinley's suggestion that she take this holiday in Queensland. Her father had been a doctor and Doc McKinley his associate. He had made all the arrangements, booking her into Glen Rose at Peregian Beach just sixteen kilometres from Noosa. 'Think of it, Eden,' he had said. 'The warm blue waters of the Pacific Ocean right at your front door. Queensland is the "Sunshine State". While you're basking in that warm tropical sun spare me a thought while I shiver under Melbourne's grey wintry skies.' He had given her an encouraging smile. 'We've done what we can for you here. The rest is up to you. Get out into that sun. Go swimming, get plenty of fresh air and exercise and pretty soon your muscles will be working properly again. You'll come back a new woman!'

And she had done what the doctor had ordered and had established a routine for herself. Breakfast at eight and then a swim in the pool. Lunch followed by a rest and another swim. Dinner. Bed. *And her nightmares!*

There was a small balcony off the bedroom of her unit and through the sliding glass doors was a clear view of the ocean. The water had an almost turquoise hue today and the rolling waves looked like fluffy white clouds scattered on top. A pathetically sad smile lifted the corners of her mouth. Her family would have loved this place.

After breakfast Eden decided she would go down to the beach. She had been at the resort for over a week and hadn't ventured past the pool.

Her legs were still very stiff and although the physiotherapists at the hospital had assured her she had made excellent progress she sometimes wondered if she wouldn't always walk with a limp.

Although still relatively early the beach was swarming with holiday makers, tanned bodies glistening with sun-tan lotion as they basked under the bright sun. Eden discarded her beach robe on the white sand and stood at the water's edge watching the clear ripples splash against her ankles. Children frolicked on either side of her while adventurous teenagers rode gigantic waves to shore. Mothers gently dipped their babies while fathers tossed squealing youngers into the softly swirling surf.

A familiar laughter made her stiffen. That was her father laughing! The laugh was full of life and merriment and Eden turned to see a tall slender grey-haired man race into the surf followed by two blonde girls in their teens. A brown-haired woman with attractive streaks of grey came after them, smiling fondly at the antics of her husband and daughters while cautiously testing the temperature of the water with her toes. Just like her own mother had always done. The family could have been *her* family and the grief returned with such force Eden felt she had been dealt a fatal blow to her stomach.

In agony she watched them. She couldn't seem to tear her eyes away. The father was teasing the girls while at the same time coaxing his pretty wife to do some body surfing. Only when the family started to regard Eden with amused curiosity, as she openly stared at them, did she finally leave the edge of the water and with her beach robe slung over her shoulder, walk blindly down the seemingly endless stretch of beach.

A dog barked. Eden looked up. She had walked to the end of the beach where casuarina trees and giant coconut palms grew among huge black boulders which jutted out to form a point. The dog barked again. Eden shaded her eyes with her hand searching for the owner of the sound. Then she saw him. A huge German Shepherd with black and brown markings stood on the point, his regal head turned towards her. Nimbly he picked his way over the rocks making his way towards where she quietly stood.

The beach was deserted, no holiday makers here. Having a healthy respect for large, unknown dogs she should have felt quite frightened. But she was too numb inside to feel anything, even fear. She stared solemnly down at the huge beast as he sat quietly in front of her, his brown eyes as grave as hers.

Slowly she stretched out her arm and placed her hand on his handsome head. 'Hi, fellow,' she said softly, noticing how well-groomed and fit he was. Whoever owned him certainly took excellent care of him. 'Where do you live, eh?'

The dog thumped his tail and barked, rising on his haunches. He ran towards the tree-lined bank and then came immediately back letting her know he expected her to follow. Eden hesitated, but only for a moment. It was a long walk back to the resort and she could do with a rest. It would be shady up there with all those huge tress. The dog barked again and Eden followed.

But the dog had no intention of letting her rest. When she had chosen a spot under an old mango tree and was about to settle herself under it, he barked again and nuzzled her hand.

'You're a bossy old thing, aren't you,' she said

laughingly, patting his head and receiving pleasure from her action. 'What's that sound I hear?' she asked, instantly alert as an incongruous tap-tap-tapping filtered through the dense copse.

The dog became positively excited and curiosity made her follow him along a narrow, winding path which eventually led to a log cabin.

From the opened windows came the sound of a typewriter. The cabin had a cheery look about it, with wide verandahs covered by a pergola with trailing red bougainvillaea twisting its way through the boards. The front door was open and the dog marched through it. Eden heard him bark several times before the typing stopped and a chair scraped along a bare floor. Almost immediately a huge figure of a man filled the doorway. His eyes widened in surprise when he saw Eden.

'Well! Well! Well!' the man drawled in that unmistakable Queensland accent. 'What have you brought home this time, Sam?'

Sam walked over and stood beside Eden, enormously pleased that he should bring such a treasure to his master. He wagged his great bushy tail and looked adoringly up at the slender young woman whose fingers were resting lightly on his head. His master strolled towards them and looked curiously down at Eden, taking in her pale skin and the purple smudges under her eyes.

Eden thought she had never seen a man who was in better health. Easily six foot two or three he positively towered over her own height of not quite five feet five inches even if she stretched. He was dressed in black shorts and white T-shirt, the shirt making his deeply tanned skin appear almost black. His hair was black and a shade too long to be really fashionable but on him it looked exactly right. Broad shoulders tapered down to narrow hips and his legs were well muscled, covered with a fine sprinkling of dark hairs. She judged him to be in his early thirties, maybe a bit younger though not by much.

His eyes were a curious shade of green, heavily fringed with thick long lashes. She found herself wondering if anyone ever teased him about those ultra-long lashes and then decided probably not. This man looked like he wouldn't take too kindly to any brand of teasing nor did he look the sort who would invite it. His rugged masculinity would put paid to that, she guessed quite accurately.

'What's the matter, kid?' he growled. 'Lost?'

Eden flushed at the use of the colloquialism, bringing a pretty glow to her pale cheeks. She straightened her shoulders and eyed him squarely, thinking as she did how pleasant his voice had sounded. Gruff but gentle.

'No, I'm not lost,' she answered, looking down at Sam. 'I'm afraid your dog led me here. I'm sorry I disturbed you.'

His green eyes narrowed shrewdly. 'Sam doesn't usually bring *people* home,' he said accusingly, making Eden feel she was a crowd instead of one. 'Why do you suppose he brought you?'

Again she flushed. 'I don't really know.' She looked down at Sam's expectant face. His black ears were pricked forward and his tail was brushing back and forth across the sandy path. He licked her hand. Eden glanced back at the stranger who was regarding her like she was some sort of oddity. She felt the hairs on the nape of her neck stiffen. This handsome man was altogether too arrogant. 'I guess he thought I would *like* it here,' she answered with the faintest trace of sarcasm in her voice.

The man's mouth curved into something resembling a smile. 'And do you?' he surprised Eden by asking.

She looked beyond him to the cabin, at the opened door and windows. The sweet scent of frangipani drifted to her nostrils and in the umbrella trees colourful parrots nibbled at clusters of red flower-like berries. Bees hummed in the jasmine vines which were just starting to open their tiny white petals, spilling their heady scent to merge with the frangipani blossoms.

Colour was everywhere, from the overpoweringly aggressive bougainvillaea which threatened to pull down the boards of the pergola to the golden allamanda which rested next to the scarlet blossoms of the West African tulips. Bush canaries darted between branches of the lillypillies and beyond the mango trees, the figs, the stringy barks and the graceful palms was the ocean, sun glistening like precious jewels against the soft tropical blue. It was all so indescribably beautiful and just being here, standing on this wild soil with its network of trees and vines and shrubs, made her feel *alive*! She drew in her breath and regarded him with solemn grey eyes.

'It's wild and wonderful,' she answered quietly, her voice revealing just how much she really did like it. Sam nuzzled her hand to remind her to continue patting him.

'Wild and wonderful,' the man drawled thoughtfully, his green eyes alight with amusement. 'That's precisely how *I* feel about the place.'

Eden merely nodded and turned her attention back to the dog. Yes, of course he would like such a wild untamed place she was thinking but she wondered if he knew how fortunate he was to have such a magnificent dog. Perhaps she should consider buying a dog. It would be someone to talk to, a companion to fill in the lonely hours. Sam leaned closer as if sensing she needed his support. None of this was lost on the man who was watching with curious amusement.

'You and Sam seem to be pretty good friends,' he remarked casually, but his green eyes were keenly watchful as she shifted from one foot to the other. 'He doesn't normally take to strangers but then perhaps you're not a stranger. Perhaps you've met several times on the beach, gone for walks, um?'

Eden straightened and tucked her blonde hair behind her ears and then shoved her hands into the pockets of her pale blue beach robe. He was probing and she couldn't really blame him. At the same time she didn't wish to reveal anything about herself.

'Oh, no,' she replied smoothly. 'Today is the first time Sam and I have met. He's a beautiful dog. You must be very proud of him.'

'He's a rogue and he knows it,' the man said and Eden heard the affection in his voice. His startling green eyes swept over her, boldly appraising her slender form not entirely concealed by the short and rather skimpy beach robe. Eden ignored those penetrating eyes while instinct told her she should leave.

'Well, I enjoyed his company,' she said sincerely, giving Sam a final pat before turning to follow the sandy path back to the beach. ' 'Bye, now.'

'What's the rush?' the man stopped her by asking. 'It's a hot day. How about a cold drink?'

Eden turned back to face him and was struck once more at how devastatingly handsome this stranger was and how easy it would be for him to charm the skin off a snake! She certainly wasn't going to be enticed to enter his cabin with its secluded surroundings.

'Thanks just the same but I really must be going.'

A few quick strides and the man was standing in front of her. Eden's eyes swept up to meet his and she was struck by the almost hypnotic power his own eyes held for her.

'You're hot and you look tired and you certainly shouldn't be wandering about without a hat.' He took her arm and Eden knew there was no way out but to allow him to bet her that drink. After all, she thought rather ruefully, Queenslanders are known for their hospitality. Still, she was glad to see Sam walking beside her.

'I'll just sit here under the pergola. It's cool and shady.'

'Nonsense!' the man growled, leading her through the door. 'It's much cooler in here and the chairs are far more comfortable. Sit wherever you choose while I get the drinks.'

The cabin was definitely cooler with the pergola trailing around all sides providing shade and allowing windows to be left open to catch the refreshing sea breezes. The walls were the same pine as outside and the huge room was sparsely furnished with old but comfortable looking furniture. At one end of the room was a large table and on this sat an old, battered typewriter, several books and a pile of paper which he must have been working on when Sam alerted him to his intruder. Behind the table, the wall was lined from ceiling to floor with shelves laden with books.

The polished floors were bare and the room had

a lived-in appearance, not completely untidy but
pretty close to it. It was obvious to Eden that this
was a man's domain and she guessed it was the
stranger's intent to keep it that way. There was
absolutely no sign of a woman's touch and she
wondered why this should please her.

On the other side of the room a servery
separated the kitchen from the living-room and
Eden could see him pouring juice into two tall
glasses, topping them up with ice. She sat in one of
the over-stuffed chairs and studied the room some
more. The windows were entirely without curtains
and through the maze of trees, shrubs and bushes
there was a panoramic view of the rolling blue
waters of the ocean. The setting was truly idyllic, a
tropical paradise with total privacy.

Sam had followed his master to the kitchen area
but now returned to stretch by Eden's legs. Almost
automatically she reached down and patted him
while both listened to the man whistling a cheery
tune which blended smoothly with the distant
sound of waves splashing across the sandy shores.
A deep feeling of peace washed over her and she
fought the almost irresistible urge to close her eyes
and . . . *sleep!*

Sleep! The one thing she hadn't had much of
since the accident. Since she had learned the tragic
news of her family's deaths, when the nightmares
had started with apparently no end. Across the
room was a door and she guessed it must be his
bedroom and that he probably slept like a baby
the whole night through. She moved closer to the
edge of her chair terrified she might fall asleep and
thinking how ironic that the one time she felt she
could sleep, she wasn't able to. She blinked her
eyes and rubbed them and while she was doing this

she didn't see him cross the room with a tray holding their drinks and a plate of cheese and crackers. His bare feet made no noise on the polished floors and although he was a huge man he moved with the grace of a jungle cat and his eyes were every bit as keen. He had watched her struggle to stay awake but said nothing as he placed the tray on a table beside her and handed her a glass of juice.

'This is delicious!' she remarked after drinking thirstily and emptying half the glass. 'I've never tasted anything quite like it.'

'My own special recipe,' he chuckled, passing a cracker heaped with cheese. 'I make it up each morning with fruit from the property. Mango, paw-paw, oranges, limes ... whatever happens to be in season and there's always something.' He waited until she had finished her cheese and cracker before announcing, 'I'm Joshua Saunders and, as I never forget a pretty face, you must be new around here.'

'Eden Baines,' she introduced herself, flushing a little at the idle compliment. A year ago she would have accepted it as part of the norm but she knew she was far too thin to be really attractive and although she dutifully prepared herself three good meals a day she had little appetite and most of what she cooked went to waste. 'I'm staying at a resort down the beach from here. The Glen Rose.'

'Ah, yes, the Glen Rose. Expensive from what I hear.'

'I guess so.'

He eyed her shrewdly between lowered lids. 'Holidaying with friends? Family?'

Eden shifted in her chair. 'No ... no, I'm on my own.'

'How long are you staying?'

'I'm booked in for a month.'

'You don't sound very happy about it.'

Eden had been toying with a few crumbs on the plate but now her eyes flew to his face. This man, this Joshua Saunders, was far too discerning for her liking. She rose to her feet, her stiff muscles robbing her of the grace ten years of ballet had given her and which only time could restore. 'I've taken up enough of your time and I really must be going.'

He stood up as well and once more she was overwhelmed by his height. She felt small and terribly vulnerable as he gazed down at her, his green eyes darkened by the shadow of his lashes. There was an aura of strength about him that had nothing to do with his obvious physical capabilities. The strong line of his jaw, the firm full mouth, the quiet manner in which he seemed to look inside her very soul. She felt he knew and understood her better than she did herself which was absolutely ridiculous considering she had only just met the man.

'Sam can walk you back to the resort,' he said and Eden felt a small stab of disappointment that he should so readily agree to her departure. Sam's tail thumped at the mention of his name and he sprang to his feet eager to be part of any action.

'Thanks, I'd like that,' she said, following Sam out the door only to stand on the verandah reluctant to leave. Dappled sun filtered through the bougainvillaea covering the pergola and rested on her cheeks. She took a deep breath savouring the heady scents of the tropical bush. 'Thank you for the snack,' she said softly, feeling suddenly very shy. 'I really enjoyed it.'

'Hold on,' he said gruffly, 'and I'll get you a hat.' He ducked into the cabin and returned seconds later with a wide brimmed straw hat and placed it squarely on her smooth cap of shining blonde hair. The hat was far too large and fell over her eyes. She pushed it back and laughed, her sudden gaiety completely transforming her features, making her suddenly very beautiful and not seem quite so delicate.

He grinned down at her, teeth flashing white against the tanned hue of his skin. A long finger reached out to lift her chin and she was forced to meet the startling brilliance of those incredibly green eyes. Eyes which fascinated her with their curious mixture of amusement and mockery; friendly but at the same time, challenging. He boldly studied her face, resting a fraction too long on her faintly trembling lips before he finally withdrew his hand and stepped back from her, hands resting on his hips in typically arrogant fashion.

'It suits you,' he said unexpectedly. 'Definitely high fashion.'

Eden chuckled and put her hand up to the wide brim. 'Oh, sure,' she scoffed, her eyes luminous instead of haunted. 'With a piece of straw between my teeth I could probably pass off as Tom Sawyer.' She removed the hat and held it out to him but he refused to take it, saying, 'This is the hottest part of the day and your skin is so fair. I'd hate to see it covered in freckles!'

Eden felt a deep flush creeping across her cheeks. Was he always so complimentary to everyone he met or did he really mean the things he said, she wondered. She decided he was just naturally suave. Still, it boosted her morale no end at a time she needed it most. First he had said she was pretty and now he had commented on her fair skin which had always been one of her best features.

'Well, I'm sure *that* won't happen with this on my head,' she said lightly, placing the hat back on her head. 'It's better than an umbrella.'

She enjoyed her walk back to the resort, taking her time out of necessity and chatting with Sam along the way, both of them with their feet in the cool water. Sam only accompanied her half way, refusing to venture where the tourists were out in full force. 'All right,' she told him. 'I realise you don't like to mix with mere tourists, that you are indeed a snob just like I suspect your master is, but I shall forgive you all the same. Off you go, then. Go back to Joshua.'

But Sam sat on his haunches refusing to budge and it came to her that he intended watching her the rest of the way to make certain she came to no harm. She tickled behind his ears. 'All right, fellow, I get the message!'

When she got to the path which turned in to the resort, Sam was a mere speck in the distance and even though she was certain he couldn't possibly still see her, she gave him a wave. It was only then that he got up and made his way back to the cabin.

The next day Eden decided she must return Joshua's hat to him. She had noticed several lying about the place but this one was probably his favourite and it was only right that she return his favourite hat. He had probably missed it that very morning while gathering fruit for his special fruit juice.

Dressed in yellow shorts, a white T-shirt and a hat of her own, a feminine white straw with yellow

band, she made her way back to the cabin. The
door was closed and there was no sound of a
typewriter coming from the opened windows. She
peeked in and everything was much the same as
before only the cabin was unmistakably empty.
She walked around to the back where she had seen
an old pick-up truck parked the day before but it
was gone. It was only then that she admitted to
herself how much she had been looking forward to
seeing Joshua Saunders again, and how foolish she
had been not to anticipate that he might not be
home. Obviously Sam had gone with him because
the great dog was nowhere to be seen and Eden
knew he would have greeted her by now had he
been anywhere close by.

She would wait fifteen minutes and if they
weren't back by then, she would leave. Fifteen
minutes passed and she gave them another fifteen
but when she had been there close to an hour the
lengthening shadows told her she had better head
back for the resort. Night fell quickly at Noosa
and she didn't want to be walking along the beach
in the dark. Swallowing her disappointment and
with Joshua's hat still in her hands, Eden made her
way back to the resort. She decided to return early
next morning to make certain she caught him
before he left for the day.

Joshua was having a snack when Eden knocked
softly on the kitchen door. He looked up and
made no attempt to mask his surprise at seeing her
there. 'Come in,' he invited, pushing himself away
from the table and crossing to the door. What
brings you here so early in the morning?' he asked,
opening the screened door to let her in. 'It's barely
ten o'clock.' And he glanced at his watch and
frowned impatiently.

'I'm not staying,' Eden hurriedly assured him knowing he must have lots to do. 'I came yesterday but you weren't here.' She held out the hat. 'I'm returning the hat you so kindly lent me.'

He frowned down at her. Tiny beads of perspiration clung to her top lip and her hair was damp clinging to the sides of her cheeks.

'You shouldn't have walked all this way,' he growled, taking the hat and tossing it on a chair.

'Oh, I didn't mind,' she hastily assured him. 'It's good exercise.'

'Not under a hot sun it isn't. This is the warmest part of the day. If you must go traipsing about do it around five in the morning or late afternoon.'

'I . . . I was worried about your hat. I thought you might be needing it.'

'You said you were here yesterday.'

Eden nodded. 'Yes, that's right.'

'Why didn't you leave the hat then? Why come all the way back?'

'Yes, I can see I should have. In fact I was going to but . . .' Her voice trailed off. *But I wanted to see you again!*

'But you didn't want to miss another opportunity of getting heat stroke, right?'

'I'm sorry I bothered you,' Eden returned stiffly. 'I can see I worried about your hat for nothing. Foolish of me for wanting to see it safely returned.'

They glared at each other for several seconds and then the expression on both their faces softened and the air cleared of the electrifying tension.

'Had breakfast?' he asked.

'Yes, thanks.'

'The coffee is freshly brewed. Like a cup?'

'That would be nice. Thank you.'

He pulled out a chair and cleared it of the magazines it was holding and Eden sat down, watching while he poured coffee into two mugs.

'Tell me about the accident,' he said casually as he stirred his coffee. He had taken the chair across from her and Eden stared at him, shocked by the bluntness of the question so casually asked. He might have been asking about the weather, or the time of day. He might have been asking about anything and she could have told him but she could never tell him about the accident.

He looked up from his coffee and saw the pain his question had provoked. He pushed his mug away, annoyed with himself that he had bothered to ask her about it. 'I knew there must have been an accident; the limp, the way you hold the mug with stiffened fingers.'

'I prefer not to discuss the accident,' she said quietly. 'I . . . I'm trying to put it behind me, make a new start.' She didn't bother asking how he knew she had been in an accident. It was something people seemed to sense and already at the resort she had been subjected to a few well-meaning remarks and offers of assistance with lounge chairs at the pool and that sort of thing. Sometimes she wondered if it wasn't her limp as much as her 'hospital pallor' which gave her away.

'Fair enough,' he agreed, picking up his mug and draining it. 'I'll give you a lift back to the resort.' He got up from his chair. 'Take your time while I stack these dishes in the dishwasher.'

Eden got up and carried her mug to the dishwasher. 'There's no need to drive me back. I prefer walking and the sun doesn't bother me. Actually, I'm trying to get a Queensland tan.'

'Just sit tight.' He growled the command. 'I'll be through here in a few minutes.'

She watched him loading the dishwasher and she ached to help but felt her assistance wouldn't be appreciated. It was obvious he was impatient to get rid of her, to get on with his work. From where she stood, Eden could see his desk and she noticed the pile of paper he had been working on had grown in size. The lounge area was fairly littered with work manuals and reference books. It must be difficult, she thought, to cook your own meals, clean up and keep a place tidy while you worked in the place at the same time.

'What you need,' she said impulsively, 'is a live-in housekeeper.'

He shut the door of the dishwasher and turned it on. 'Think so?' he drawled, green eyes glittering. 'Would you like the job?'

She knew he was teasing and she entered into the mood. 'Sure, why not?'

'You mean you would move in?' He snapped his fingers. 'Just like that?'

Was he teasing? Eden felt her heart skip several beats and then hammer against her ribs. She licked her lips and said rather nervously. 'Of course not . . . I was only teasing!'

CHAPTER TWO

SHE felt she could put her finger up and pluck a star from the sky. There were trillions of them, sparkling, shining, densely scattered against the thick black velvet of the night.

A soft breeze fanned her cheeks and gently lifted the silky tresses of her hair. The ever moving surf pounded away in the darkness, the white caps fluorescent under the waning noon. Eden sat as still as a small child in Sunday school, listening to the sounds of the night.

She had been to the cabaret. Cabarets were one of the more popular functions at the resort and took place each Saturday night. She hadn't wanted to go, hadn't even considered going but at last had given in to the most persistent of her many admirers. Before the accident she had more than her fair share of boyfriends but none of them had ever treated her with kid gloves the way she was being handled now. Like she wasn't a real person! Like she was a fragile doll. Her loss of weight made her seem delicate and this in itself brought out the masculine desire to protect and to hover around her like she was in danger of breaking.

She had stood it for an hour and then had quietly excused herself, glad to escape from the jarring music, the cigarette smoke, the unnatural attention.

Not that she minded having the usual courtesies extended to her. Doors opened, chair pulled out, that sort of thing. It was the *manner* in which it was done which nettled her. She wasn't an invalid and didn't take kindly to being treated like one.

Joshua Saunders certainly didn't treat her as one! In fact she doubted if he ever noticed her limp. She hadn't seen him for over a week but found herself constantly thinking about him. Now, as she sat on the patio settee outside her unit in the soft moonlit night, a sweet smile lifted the corners of her tender mouth. He hadn't liked it when she had insisted on walking back to the resort under the hot sun. A sun which she thrived on and felt she couldn't get enough of.

In the end they had reached a compromise. She had sat still while he applied a sticky white paste to her nose and cheeks. It had kept her free of sunburn all right, but it had taken ages to scrub off when she got back to the unit. And it hadn't been easy to sit still when the most handsome man she had ever come across, or was ever likely to again, had been so heart rendingly close to her as he applied the paste.

Incredible how gentle those big hands had been, she thought now, for easily the hundredth time. Spasms had rippled through her body and her heart had somersaulted in her chest. Had he noticed the effect he had on her? Her pale cheeks coloured because she was certain he had!

Eden shifted restlessly on the settee and sighed. Too bad, that. If he hadn't noticed then she would have felt free to visit him again. But to go now, when it was obvious to both of them that he held a wild attraction for her, would be the same as deliberately walking into a lion's den!

So she had done the next best thing. Each day she had met Sam on the beach and together they had walked up the path and under the shelter and protection of a huge mango tree, they had listened to some beautiful music. The sound of Joshua typing!

She had pictured him sitting at his table with the battered old typewriter, long, brown fingers skipping across the keys. What was he working on? A thesis, perhaps? There had certainly been enough reference books around to make this a possibility. Sometimes the typing had been fierce and fast and she knew whatever he was working on was coming easily. Other times it would be almost painfully slow and she knew he was experiencing difficulties. Sometimes the typing would come to a complete halt and she found herself holding her breath until it resumed. These sessions left her feeling exhausted as if she had indeed been sitting in on a symphony that affected her every nerve. She had felt part of him, secretly sharing his life. And at night, waiting for sleep, which was always a long time coming, it was his face which swam before her eyes and not her family's. Eden leaned back and closed her eyes, mouth still lifted in a smile.

She hadn't met Sam today. She had told him yesterday that she would be busy ... her laundry to do, ironing, letters to write. But she would meet him tomorrow and her smile deepened at the thought of the juicy bone in the fridge which was to be his treat. Perhaps she shouldn't be feeding him ...

'Hullo, Eden.' A deep voice from the shadows interrupted her reverie. Her head snapped up and she sprang forward in her seat, hand flying to her chest as she peered into the darkness. She would recognise that voice anywhere only she couldn't believe that it would actually be him.

Joshua stepped out of the shadows and walked across the tiled patio to sit next to her on the settee. Dressed in black slacks, crisp white shirt and a white jacket flung casually over his shoulder, he fairly made her head spin at the handsome picture he made.

'Hullo, Joshua,' she returned, her voice revealing her inner turmoil. 'You gave me a fright. I . . . I wasn't expecting you.'

'Sorry if I frightened you.' He took her small hand and held it. Shivers raced up her arm and she snatched it away.

'You . . . you didn't really frighten me,' she said breathlessly. 'It's just that I . . . I wasn't expecting . . . anyone.'

'I did scare you,' he said caringly. 'You're trembling.'

'Am I? Yes, yes I suppose I am. It's so dark . . . one hears of such terrible things happening. I guess you did frighten me . . . a little.'

He smiled down at her and slipped his arm around her shoulders drawing her close to him. 'There, now,' he said softly, his voice sounding seductively husky in the darkness. 'Calm yourself. It's only me.'

Only him! She had spent the past week thinking about him. He had crowded her thoughts from morning to night. She had spent the evenings going over every word they had spoken to each other. *Only him!*

'Yes, silly of me to be so startled.' She jumped up. 'Now that you're here may I get you something? Coffee? Tea?' *Me?* Good grief! She had almost said that aloud! Get a grip on yourself, girl, she chided herself. Stop behaving as though you thought you would never see him again.

He rose easily to his feet, his green eyes alight with amusement. 'Coffee would be fine,' he said, adding, 'Are you quite sure you can manage?'

She didn't answer. Instead she turned and slipped through the patio door and into the lounge. He followed and looked around at the spotlessly clean room. Not a thing was out of place. Not a magazine, not even a speck of dust could be seen. He grinned and placed his jacket over the arm of a stiff-backed chair.

'Not like my place, eh? No wonder you thought I needed a housekeeper. You're certainly a very tidy person. It almost looks like no one lives here.'

'Well, actually I'm not in much.'

His eyes swept down her slender body. She was still wearing the dress she had worn to the cabaret, a simple blue frock. It came to her that it was the first time either had seen the other in anything but shorts or a beach jacket.

'Been out?' he asked in a drawl.

'The cabaret . . . here at the resort.' She took a deep breath. 'You?'

'A party . . . down the road from here.'

'Was it fun?'

He shrugged his broad shoulders. 'No, it was rather dull.' He searched her face. 'How was the cabaret?'

'It was all right. The music was loud.'

'You look tired. Are you all right?'

'Yes, I'm fine. A bit of a headache, that's all.'

'Do you think you should have gone to the cabaret?'

Eden smiled. 'Sure, why not?'

Joshua frowned. 'You didn't come around today. I thought you might be ill.'

Eden stared at him . . . then her cheeks flooded

with colour as realisation set in. 'Come around?' she echoed in a strained voice. 'Where?'

'To my place!' A wicked gleam shone from his eyes. 'To where you and Sam picnic under the mango tree.'

'You . . . you *knew* about that?'

He nodded, amused by her discomfort. 'Of course, I knew. Why didn't you come up to the cabin?'

'I . . .' She bit her lip and smoothed her hands down the front of her dress. How embarrassing to think he knew all along that she was at the bottom of his property. What had he thought? What was he thinking now? She might have known nothing would escape those watchful eyes. Eyes which seemed capable of seeing in the dark and certainly capable of looking through thick tropical bush to where she had sat with Sam. Why, she hadn't even been able to see the cabin, had only heard the sound of his typewriter. 'I didn't wish to bother you,' she finally explained. 'Besides,' she went on, 'I suppose if you wanted my company you would have given me a shout.' She smiled to let him know her words were spoken in jest.

'You've always been so eager to get away from me I decided it wouldn't be wise to, ah, give you a shout.' His smile was charming. 'But I'm glad to see you're fine. Haven't suffered sunstroke yet but I see you're working on it. Your nose is burnt. The skin is peeling.'

She put her hand up to gingerly touch her nose. Trust him to notice such a thing. 'It doesn't hurt,' she said and then suddenly became angry. 'Is there anything else you wish to mention? Good heavens! First you accuse me of spying on you, then . . .'

His deep chuckle washed over her effectively silencing her. 'Spying?' he growled. 'I didn't say you were *spying*.' His green eyes widened in mock horror. '*Were* you spying?'

Colour seared her cheeks, darker than any sunburn. 'You know I wasn't. It just so happens that you own the only shade trees on the beach. With all your remarks about keeping out of the sun, I . . .'

The sharp jangle of the telephone stopped her. She looked nervously down at it. The hour was late and she wasn't expecting a call. Joshua's black brows rose questioningly. 'Shall I get it?'

But even as he spoke he had lifted the receiver and was speaking quietly into it. He held the 'phone out to Eden. 'It's a Dr McKinley ringing from Melbourne. Do you want to take the call?'

'Oh, yes, of course,' she said with relief, wondering why she had been so edgy. She held the receiver to her ear. 'Hi, Doc,' she said softly.

'Eden! I've been trying to reach you all night. Are you all right?'

'I'm fine, Doc. I was out earlier . . . to a cabaret.' She knew the old doctor would like hearing she had been dancing.

'Good! Good! Didn't I tell you Glen Rose was the place to go?'

'Yes,' she smiled into the mouthpiece, 'and you were right. I'm having a terrific time.'

'That's my girl. Now tell me, Eden, who was that man who answered the 'phone? Sounded rather nice.'

Eden looked across at Joshua who was making no effort to conceal the fact he was listening to every word. 'Oh, him,' she said with a bored air. 'Just a man I met. Lives on the beach.'

Doc McKinley's voice roared from the earpiece. 'Not a beach boy, Eden! Not one of those *surfies*!'

'Just one minute and I'll ask him.' She turned wide eyes towards Joshua. 'Do you surf?' she asked sweetly which brought an answering smirk. She turned back to the telephone. 'I don't think he has time, Doc,' she said. 'He spends most of his time typing.'

'Typing?' Doc asked, puzzled. 'Did you say "typing", Eden?'

'Yes, he's practically a hermit. You know the type. Lives alone . . . bare floors . . . no curtains. His only companion is a dog. A real loner.'

'You shouldn't befriend someone like that, Eden. I'm surprised you're entertaining him. I don't like it.'

'Oh, he's perfectly harmless, Doc. He just came around to see if I was all right. You see, I've made friends with his *dog*, not *him*!' She pretended not to notice Joshua's murderous scowl. After assuring Doc that she was eating properly and doing her exercises he finally let her go.

'So you're from Melbourne,' Joshua stated when she hung up the 'phone. 'What can a girl from Melbourne teach a harmless hermit?'

Her laugh was shaky. 'Oh, don't be such a prude. I was joking. Surely you realised . . .'

He grabbed her to him, smiling into her startled grey eyes. She opened her mouth to protest and he bent his head and kissed her. She struggled against him but he only held her tighter, his strong arms like steel bands across her back. A wild excitement surged through her but she willed herself not to let him know, forcing herself to remain still and uncaring in his arms. When he released her, green eyes alight with amused mockery, Eden raised her hand and rubbed her mouth.

'How *dare* you!' she gasped, more outraged than the action warranted.

'Now who's the prude?' he asked carelessly, slipping his hands into his pockets and grinning down at her. 'What's the matter, small stuff? Haven't you been kissed before?'

She glared up at him, heart still hammering in her chest as she fought the almost overwhelming desire to strike him. She took a deep breath. 'Yes . . . but never by a barbarian!'

His appreciative roar of laughter took her by surprise. She had intended to wound, not amuse him. She should have known better than to try and match swords with this . . . this heathen! She brushed past him, chin raised defiantly.

'Coffee, wasn't it?' she tossed over her shoulder as she entered the small kitchen adjoining the lounge. He glanced at his wristwatch and for a terrifying second she thought he would say he had to leave. And she didn't want to be alone. She could handle the days but the nights seemed to stretch on endlessly. He caught her expression; saw the wistful loneliness, the deep hurt in the shadows of her eyes.

'Yes, coffee.' He followed her into the small kitchen and watched while she filled the kettle and plugged it into the wall socket. Her hands were trembling as she got out cups and saucers and placed them on the shining counter top. Already she knew how he liked his coffee—milk, two sugars. She wished she had some cake to serve him.

'I've got some biscuits,' she said. 'Not home-made but they're still rather nice.' She went to the cupboard and pulled out a packet of strawberry creams, holding them up for inspection. He shook his head. 'No, thanks. The coffee will do.' She put them back.

The kettle boiled and she reached for it but his

hand had already closed over the handle. 'I'll do it,' he said quietly and Eden snatched her hand back and held it with her other in an effort to still them. She was shaking like a leaf. She hoped he hadn't noticed. Why, she was behaving like an awkward schoolgirl and knew she could blame his kiss for that *and* for the burning sensation she still felt. It was all she could do to keep her fingers from touching her mouth.

'This is a nice place,' he casually remarked as he drank his coffee.

'Yes,' she agreed, her eyes lowered on the cup in front of her.

He watched her closely. 'You're sure you're happy here?'

Her eyes flew to his face. 'Of course. What kind of question is that?'

Joshua shrugged. 'You don't *seem* happy. Usually young people holiday with friends or family.'

Eden turned her face away. 'I . . . I like being alone,' she said, swallowing hard. 'Just like you. You're alone at the cabin.'

He shook his head. 'It's not the same and you know it. I've elected for total privacy.'

'And what makes you think I haven't?' she challenged, feeling a lump forming in her throat.

'That 'phone call from Melbourne. Why was your doctor checking up on you?'

'He's a friend. Friends do things like that,' she flared, feeling the conversation was getting dangerous.

'What are you hiding, Eden? Why can't you discuss your accident? It helps to . . .'

Eden jumped up. 'Please!' she begged, her voice catching. 'I've told you before . . . I'm here to *forget* the accident!'

His voice was steady. 'How can you forget something which has happened to you, Eden? You're hurting so badly I can *feel* it. You shouldn't be alone. You need to talk out your feelings.'

'I don't!' She raised her hand to her throbbing temple. *'I don't!'*

Joshua leaned back in his chair, green eyes narrowed as he watched her. 'Who was killed? Your boyfriend? A fiancé? A lover, perhaps?'

Her face was a deathly white. 'How could you be so cruel?' she choked.

'So I was right,' he said quietly. 'Must have been rough but surely your family could have seen you through it...? You're young ... you have your whole life ahead of you. Someday you will learn to forget. One hour at a time, a day, a week...'

'Stop!' Her whole head was throbbing. Never had the pain been so intense. She looked at him through tears, her voice a sob. 'How could you be so *insensitive*?' she cried out. 'Only when you've lost what I have lost, God forbid, will you begin to understand how I feel.'

He wasn't in the least disturbed. 'I'm not disputing the fact you've suffered, Eden, because it's obvious you have. What I can't understand is why you've given in so easily; why you haven't fought harder for your own recovery. The grave claims us all in good enough time, so while we're here we should make the most of it.'

Her body was trembling, her face ashen. 'Get out!' she whispered hoarsely. 'Get out!'

He took another swallow of his coffee, then ran his thumb around the rim of the cup. He ignored her whispered plea. 'Leave you alone?' he enquired softly. 'Like your family have done? Like your so-called doctor friend? You're a long way from home, Eden. Why have they sent you up here? You need support right now, not isolation.' He got up and circled the table, putting his hands on her shoulders. She felt so thin. He could feel the small, fine bones ... She looked up at him, grey eyes swimming. Hastily she reached up but she couldn't wipe the tears away. He slipped his arms around her but she darted out of his hold. A sombre look came into his eyes; eyes which up until now had been heavy with concern.

'Don't touch me!' she said.

'I was merely trying to comfort you,' he growled in a low voice. He took a deep breath and let it out slowly. 'He can't watch you from the grave!'

'Don't talk like that! Don't ever talk like that to me *again*!'

He crossed the room and picked up his jacket, swinging it over his shoulder. 'Are you coming around to the cabin tomorrow?' he asked and his voice sounded tired.

Eden ran her hands through her hair and straightened her shoulders. The man had to be mad asking a question like that after the horrible things he had just said to her.

'Most definitely not!'

'Sam will miss you,' he said softly. 'He'll go looking for you.'

'I'm sure you can explain the situation to him,' she answered stiffly.

They stood looking at each other. It came to Eden that he might be sorry for the things he had said to her and well he should be she thought without satisfaction. But the set of his handsome features, stern and without remorse told her he had felt justified in saying what he had.

'I'll try but it won't be easy.' He smiled crookedly down at her. 'Sam's got rather used to you.'

Eden said nothing. She would miss Sam and as much as she hated to admit it, she would also miss his master. The patio doors were open and Joshua turned and stepped into the shadowy darkness of the sweetly scented night.

'Wait,' she called after him. He turned, black brows arched. 'I . . . I have something for Sam,' she explained. 'A bone. I was saving it for him.'

He stepped back into the room while she hurried to the fridge, taking out Sam's treat. Quickly she wrapped it and handed it to him. He held the bulky parcel in his hand and looked at her.

'Go straight to bed, Eden,' he said gruffly. 'You look exhausted.'

Bed. Her nightmares. Snatches of sleep between horrifying dreams. Voices whispering at her, telling her . . . She put a slender hand to her head and tried to smile but failed. 'Yes, I will,' she promised wondering at his concern and wishing now she hadn't asked him to leave. 'Good night, Joshua.'

Eden spent a sleepless night going over the reasons why she hadn't told Joshua about her family. By morning she had arrived at two conclusions, neither of which were very satisfactory she had to admit as she stood by the sliding glass doors and watched the rolling blue seas. He hadn't given her a chance and she had been afraid of his pity.

Pity! There had been so much of that at the hospital. She could endure his anger, she felt sure, but not his pity. She turned away from the scene in front of her and stared at herself in the mirror. Did her suffering show? Could he really see behind the mask she had been wearing for so long, her thin veneer of so-called gaiety? But she was trying . . . trying . . . had tried so hard.

There was the sound of banging at her door. From her upstairs bedroom she could hear the loud, persistent sounds. No mistake about it. There was someone intent on breaking the door down! Eden grabbed her dressing gown and struggled into it as she quickly made her way down the stairs.

The curtains were drawn and she pulled back a corner to see Joshua's massive frame looming outside. She stared at him for several seconds before she finally pulled the curtains the rest of the way and released the catch on the doors, sliding them back.

'Wh . . . What are you doing here?' she asked, blinking against the dazzling rays of the sun which filled the room. 'I thought . . . after last night . . . I should never see you again.'

He stepped inside and closed the doors behind him. Dressed in white shorts and pale yellow golf shirt he looked incredibly fresh and handsome. It was obvious to Eden that he at least had enjoyed a good night's sleep. While she had tossed and turned, going over the things he had said to her, he had been sleeping soundly. The cad!

'And if I had half a brain in my head you wouldn't be seeing me again,' he growled, peering down into her small tired face. 'Get dressed and pack your belongings. You're coming with me.'

A sliver of fear sliced through her body. 'With you? Where?'

'To my cabin, where else? God knows you've

spent enough time there, you may as well move right in and put yourself to good use.'

Her fear was growing. 'Good use?' she echoed. 'What kind of good use?'

He tossed her a wicked grin. 'I'll tell you after you've packed. Now get a move on. I haven't got all day.'

She resisted the urge to remind him the day had barely begun. Instead she smiled. 'I wouldn't dream of moving in with you. How presumptuous of you to assume that I would.'

'Not at all!' He returned her smile. 'Either dress and pack or I'll do it for you!'

'Now hold on here,' she spluttered, clutching at her dressing gown. 'You can't just barge in here and order me about.'

'Can't I?' he drawled wickedly, green eyes glittering. 'What do you want me to do first? Dress you . . . or pack your things?'

'Be reasonable,' she coaxed. 'You're so busy while I . . . I would have nothing to do. I'd get in your way. You'd hate having me there.'

'Woman,' he growled, 'you'll have plenty to do. You won't have time to get in my way. Now get a move on.'

'I'm not going,' she repeated stoutly, lifting her chin defiantly. 'You can't make me.'

'Move!' he roared.

Eden jumped. 'Don't shout at me!' she flared, taking a hasty step backwards. 'Just who do you think you are?' she dared to add.

Even as she said the words she knew she had made a mistake. His hand lashed out and grabbed both of hers pulling her towards him. 'That was just the challenge I needed,' he rasped angrily, green eyes narrowed into menacing slits. 'Why I should concern myself about you in the first place . . .' His voice trailed off at the look in her eyes and he dropped her hands. He dragged his hand wearily through the thick scrub of his hair. 'Don't argue, Eden. Just do as I say. I have your best interests at heart.'

She placed her hands on her hips. 'What best interests?' she demanded to know. 'What did you mean when you said I would have plenty to do?'

'Well,' he drawled and he had the audacity to grin, 'you remember how we discussed my housekeeping problems?' Eden nodded. 'I've hired several housekeepers in the past but I've never been able to keep one for long.' His smile broadened. 'They claimed I was too hard a taskmaster, now can you believe that?'

She could believe it all right, just like she knew where this conversation was leading. She wasn't in the least surprised when he cheerfully said: 'I got to thinking last night how much you needed company and how I needed a housekeeper. You could look after things at the cabin, keep it clean and tidy . . . prepare meals . . . play with Sam. Of course I would pay you the going rate.' His smile was outrageously charming. 'How does it all sound?'

'Like you've got a few screws loose in your head!'

CHAPTER THREE

HE drove straight past the reception area and on to the highway. Eden glanced back. 'But I must book out!'

'I've already done that. They will forward your mail to my place.' He indicated an envelope on the dashboard. 'That's your refund cheque.'

'You certainly don't waste any time, do you?' she replied stiffly. 'I wonder what they're thinking.'

'Who?'

'The people at Glen Rose of course. They will think it strange that I didn't book out myself and to leave on such short notice like this. Well really no notice at all. I can't believe I'm actually sitting in your truck on my way to your place.' She glanced at his stony profile and gave an involuntary shudder. 'Pardon me for saying but I don't believe I'm going to enjoy your company.'

He didn't spare her a glance. She turned away and muttered, 'Thank goodness Sam will be there!'

Joshua's green eyes danced with wicked bright lights as he grinned down at her. Her dress, pink with white pockets, was a bit big for her and she was far too thin but there was an aura of quiet strength about her which had intrigued him from the beginning. Her blonde hair was brushed smoothly back, hugging the delicate structure of her head and falling against the slender column of her neck. His grin changed into a smile as he turned his attention back to his driving.

'Usually you don't talk so much,' he drawled, deliberately baiting her. 'I detest females who ramble on and on saying nothing in particular.'

'Well, I'm certainly not like *that*!' she declared hotly, turning to look at him. 'And I wasn't rambling. Naturally I would be concerned about the people at Glen Rose and what they would be thinking.' A pause. 'You had me packed and out of there so fast I'm not even sure what *I'm* thinking! Not to mention Doc McKinley,' she continued. 'I'll write to him immediately and explain about my job.' She shook her head. 'A housekeeper! He'll think I've gone mad!'

His chuckle washed over her making her feel good inside. 'There's nothing wrong with house-keeping. What kind of work did you do before the accident?'

Eden looked down at her hands folded neatly in her lap. 'I was in my final year of nursing,' she replied quietly.

'Well, you can go back to it someday.'

Eden shook her head. 'No, I don't think I ever will.'

'Why not?' he gently prodded, noticing the way she was wringing her hands.

She bowed her head. She had been doing her training at the same hospital as her father had worked and where she had recovered from the accident. It was the one place she felt she could never return. 'I . . . I've decided nursing isn't really for me,' she answered at last.

His black brows arched in surprise. 'After nearly completely your training? I should imagine your parents will have something to say about that!'

Eden clamped her teeth on her bottom lip. 'My parents . . .' She squeezed her eyes shut. '. . . My parents have always trusted me to make my own decisions,' she finally managed.

His eyes narrowed at the sight of her unhappy face. Eden prayed thàt he would let the matter drop and when he turned his attention back to the road she sighed her relief, which he heard but didn't comment upon. Instead he pointed out the scenery.

'I can remember when all this was bush,' he remarked and Eden looked at the ultra-modern beach homes which seemed to spring from every nook and cranny. 'Development has got out of hand over the past few years and with it the price of land has skyrocketed.'

'It's the climate,' she volunteered, grateful the conversation was on this neutral ground. 'You can't blame people for wanting to build where it's warm the year round and where there are such lovely beaches.'

With every turn the sparkling blue ocean peeped through swaying palms while the dazzling sun glittered like diamonds on the rolling surf. Grassy slopes gave way to sandy beaches fringed with casuarina trees, mossy green needles hanging from their spiky branches. The morning tide was coming in, swirling over glistening black boulders, forming frothy white pools at their bases.

'You've only seen my property from the beach side,' Joshua told her as he swung the old truck on to a narrower road, 'but this is the start of my property now. It's been selectively cleared so there are still plenty of native trees and shrubs.'

Eden stared. 'You mean *all* this beautiful land is yours?' she asked incredulously. 'It must be worth a fortune!'

He chuckled. 'Depends on what you call a

fortune but I've been offered well in excess of a
million dollars for it. It's all beach frontage on one
boundary and road on the other. It could easily
accommodate several large resorts.'

'But you would never sell?'

He shook his head. 'Never! If it happens that I
no longer like coming here then I will donate it to
the town for a wildlife park. When the land
developers get through covering everything with
concrete then at least there will be this bit of green
oasis left.'

'Glen Rose isn't all concrete,' Eden defended the
resort. 'In fact it's mostly green grass, trees and
flowering shrubs. You can't even see it from the
beach it's so nestled among the flora. Surely you
wouldn't mind selling your land for complexes like
that?'

'I will never sell,' he repeated.

'Then you mustn't need the money.' She
thought of the cabin and the sparse furnishings.
'Perhaps you could sell some of it and enlarge
your cabin.'

'What for?'

She shrugged. 'Well, I don't know. For guests
perhaps?'

'I detest guests! Besides, the cabin is bigger than
you think. You haven't seen much of it.'

They pulled up to the back of the cabin and
Eden looked at it with a great deal of satisfaction.
No wonder he would never sell she thought, as the
same feeling of peace washed over her like the first
time she had seen it. She looked up at the umbrella
trees. Parrots were nibbling at the clusters of berry
blossoms, screeching between nibbles. Sam came
bounding from around the corner and Eden
stepped from the truck to greet him.

She knelt beneath the shade of a weeping bottlebrush tree, the crimson clusters casting rosy shadows across her cheeks. 'Hi, old fellow,' she murmured against his head, thin arms stretched around his neck. 'Glad to see me, are you? Surprised too, no doubt.'

'I should run and fetch my camera,' Joshua smiled above them.

Eden looked up. 'I bet you have hundreds of photos of Sam.'

His green eyes were strangely intent as he looked down at her. 'You looked *happy*, Eden. Your eyes are usually so solemn . . .'

She rose slowly to her feet, traces of the smile still lingering in the clear grey of her beautiful eyes. 'Sam brings out the best in me,' she replied softly, caught in the powerful grip of his magnetic green eyes. Her heart which had been a frozen block since the deaths of her family lurched against her ribs, as though the searing heat from his eyes had sought it out and begun the painful process of melting it. She raised a trembling hand to her mouth. Even her lips felt strangely warm.

He took her arm. 'Come on,' he said gruffly. 'I have work to do and I want to show you where everything is so you can get started on some sort of routine.'

Her heart sank when she saw the kitchen. The table hadn't been cleared from his breakfast that morning nor had the dishes been put in the dishwasher from the night before. Up until now she had harboured the hope he craved her company as much as she did his but obviously it was her housekeeping skills he was most interested in and the kitchen alone promised a real challenge.

'I'll show you your room,' he said cheerfully,

leading her past the mess. 'It faces the ocean and even on the hottest days you'll get a refreshing breeze.'

The room he led her to was down a small hall off the kitchen. It was bright and airy and extremely pleasant with its cane furnishings and pastel colours of pink, yellow and green. The walls were the same pine as the rest of the cabin and a pale fluffy yellow rug covered the bare floor. There were also curtains she was glad to see, the pretty floral design matching the bedspread on the double four-poster bed and the cushions on the cane chairs. From the patio door she had a clear view of the brilliantly blooming garden and the rolling surf beyond. Under the shade of a flowering purple jacaranda tree Sam stretched out and quietly snoozed. A sigh of sheer contentment slipped from her parted lips.

'I'll get your cases,' Joshua said, watching her as she gazed out at the garden and at Sam. She turned and murmured her thanks and when he had gone she sat wearily on the bed. Perhaps here she would get the peace she so badly needed she thought, as her eyes swept around the room with its restful furnishings.

He returned almost immediately with her baggage, crossing the room to put the cases beside her on the bed. Eden jumped up, a guilty flush creeping across her cheeks that she had been caught sitting down on the job even though she tried to tell herself the job hadn't really begun.

'How does your room feel?' he asked considerately. 'Like it?'

'Yes, very much,' she answered honestly. 'It's a woman's room. Did you decorate it?'

His handsome mouth quirked into a smile.

'Observant little creature, aren't you?' he laughed. 'No, I didn't do it, a friend of mine did. She, ah, used to use it whenever she came visiting.'

Eden looked once more around the room and decided whoever the woman was, she certainly had a flair for decorating. 'Don't you allow her to visit anymore?' she asked innocently, thinking of all the work which must have gone into the room. The curtains, bedspread and matching cushions looked like they had been sewn by hand.

'*Allow?*' he chuckled. 'What made you use that word?'

Her fine brows arched in surprise. 'You did. You said you detested guests,' she reminded him.

'Guests, yes. The occasional guest, no. You really do think of me as a hermit don't you?' he said smilingly as he unlocked her cases and lifted the lids. 'There should be plenty of space for your clothes.' He walked with his easy stride to the built-in closets and opened the folding doors.

'Goodness!' Eden exclaimed. 'Even if I hung up my socks there would be space left over! Thank you.'

She watched as he reached into the closet and took out a garment. It was a beautiful pink satin dressing gown. He folded it across his arm and turned to her. 'If there's anything you need or can't find just let me know.'

Eden couldn't tear her eyes from the gown. Against the tanned skin of his arm, the pink satin looked seductively feminine and extremely alluring. She couldn't help but wonder about his female friend and what she looked like, was like, who owned such a beautiful garment.

'But what if she visits while I'm here?' Eden heard herself asking in a voice which sounded strained.

His black brows rose mockingly. 'What if she does?'

'Well . . .' Eden was feeling flustered. 'Well, I'm here,' she answered helplessly. 'In . . . in her room.'

His green eyes glinted down at her. 'So you are,' he returned easily, deliberately mocking her. 'But there's no need to worry. She doesn't use this room anymore.'

'Is . . . Is that *her* gown?'

'Yup. Pretty, isn't it?'

'Very.' Eden dragged her eyes up to his. 'Why doesn't she use this room?'

'Oh, Clare's a very practical person,' he stated drily, 'and in many cases so am I.' A deliberate pause while he toyed with the thin straps of the gown. 'Why use two beds when one serves the same purpose!'

'You mean you sleep with her?'

'Does that shock you?'

'Of course not!'

'But it does. I can see it in your eyes.'

Eden dropped her eyes feeling very foolish. 'I presume you're both of age,' she answered stiffly. 'I just thought,' she cleared her throat, 'I just thought it might be awkward if she came while I'm here.'

'How so?' he asked, tossing the satin gown over his shoulder, eyes alight with unconcealed amusement.

'Well . . . well, I know I wouldn't like it if I paid my boyfriend a visit and found another woman there.'

He pretended to ponder this. 'Another woman? You mean *you*?' he asked incredulously, causing a deep stain to creep across Eden's cheeks. 'But you're not another woman! You're my *housekeeper*! There's a world of difference between the two.'

Insufferable swine! she thought as she glared up at him, wondering at his bold-faced conceit. 'Yes, of course there is,' she answered with all the dignity she could muster. 'I hope you didn't think I was implying that I . . . that we . . .' She couldn't finish. How dare he deliberately twist her words and put her in this awkward situation.

'That we might become lovers?' he softly taunted, bringing an even darker stain to Eden's cheeks. 'The idea is appealing.'

Eden had difficulty breathing. She stood straighter, squarely meeting his glance. 'Not to me it isn't. I think being your housekeeper will be difficult enough.'

He laughed and Eden relaxed. She began unpacking her cases, laying her clothes neatly across the bed, hoping that he would leave.

'If it will make you feel better,' he said, 'Clare can have the room across the hall. It's smaller than this but she decorated it as well.' He watched her place several articles of clothing on top of the bureau before tugging at the drawers with her stiff fingers. A muscle worked spasmodically alongside his jaw as he watched her struggle and then stopped abruptly when the drawers were safely opened and she was placing her clothing inside.

'So you are expecting her then?' Eden asked as she hung her dresses and slacks in the closet.

He shrugged. 'Not really, although Clare does have a tendency to arrive unannounced.'

'Charming.'

An easy grin spread across his face. 'She is, rather.'

'Well, please don't feel you must keep her out of

your bed on my account. It's certainly none of my business where she sleeps.' She gave him a sideways glance. 'After all, I'm merely your housekeeper. I won't be concerning myself with any of your bachelor capers so feel free to romp and roam all you please.'

'Such generosity!' he chuckled.

She pushed the drawers shut. 'Not at all. You seemed concerned that I might not know the difference between a housekeeper and a woman. I'm only assuring you that I'm quite happy to be a housekeeper.'

'A housekeeper who happens to be a very beautiful young lady,' he said quietly, his tone unnerving her more than she cared to admit. He crossed the room and stood by the door. 'The bathroom is just down the hall.' He glanced at his watch and she saw him frown. 'Don't be much longer. I'd like to get started on my work.' He looked up. 'I'll wait for you in the lounge.'

And then he was gone. Eden waited until she heard his footsteps fade before she opened the door and made her way to the bathroom, ignoring the closed door of the other guest room as she passed it. No doubt it would never be used by the woman named Clare she thought ruefully and then told herself if Joshua and Clare were lovers it certainly was no concern of hers. She doubted they would stay away from one another merely on her account. Anyway, she could only pray that she would be long gone before Clare made one of her surprise visits. No matter what Joshua believed, Eden seriously doubted Clare would be overjoyed to find another woman under Joshua's roof!

The bathroom was lovely. With a few ferns hanging in front of the opened window it could look beautiful. Eden made a mental note to install some ferns which would be extremely attractive against the pine setting. All this place really needs is a woman's touch she thought as she bathed her hands and face and passed a brush through her simple hairstyle. She studied her reflection in the mirror and pursed her lips. She was still far too thin and the dark smudges under her eyes certainly didn't help. She pulled a face and grinned, wondering what Joshua's other housekeepers had looked like.

Joshua was sitting behind his table when Eden entered the lounge. His dark head was bent over his work and she realised now that it was a manuscript he was working on and that it had practically tripled in size since first she had seen it. She waited for him to become aware that she was in the room but so absorbed was he in his work that she finally had to draw his attention to her presence.

'Well, here I am,' she said brightly. 'Reporting for duty.'

His head shot up and she saw by his expression that he was clearly annoyed. 'Rule number one!' he snapped. 'Never disturb me when I'm working. I'm a writer,' he declared arrogantly, 'and writers don't like interruptions.'

'Well, pardon me, sir, but you did say you wanted to discuss my duties.' She flicked back her hair. 'I can always take a nap and come back later.'

He pushed himself away from the table and ran a hand through the unruly mass of his dark hair. 'No, stay. I'm sorry I yelled at you. I can be rather overbearing at times.' He smiled crookedly and her heart lurched in her chest.

'That's all right,' she said, swallowing hard. 'I'm used to men like you.'

'Men like me?'

'Doctors. Some of them like to shout at nurses.'

'And what did you do when it happened to you?'

'I ignored them,' she said pointedly and he laughed.

Eden looked at the manuscript. 'I've heard you typing. Did you type all that yourself?'

'Every damn word!'

'Why don't you dictate it and get someone to type it up for you?' she asked reasonably.

'I've tried that but if the bloody machine wasn't breaking down then the typist was! I've found it's easier to work solo.'

Eden smiled. 'Yes,' she agreed, 'I should imagine you would. I hope you weren't too hard on your typist though. I bet she was terrified of you.'

'Probably.' He shrugged his broad shoulders and grinned, grooves appearing attractively on the sides of his rugged face. Eden felt the blood rush to her cheeks and she quickly looked away, focusing her attention on the manuscript.

'Are you writing a book?' she asked.

'Yup.'

'Your first?'

'Nope.'

Her eyes swept to his face and she saw the teasing lights in his eyes. She moved closer to the table and picked up one of several carefully bound sheaves of paper. 'Are you writing your autobiography?' she asked seriously.

Joshua threw back his head and roared with laughter. 'Not yet, not now, probably not ever,' he finally got out, green eyes sparkling as he watched her standing stiffly in front of the table. 'You really don't know who I am,' he stated matter-of-factly and she got the impression that not only was he glad about this but was also secretly pleased.

'But I should?'

'Not necessarily,' he drawled. 'You've been out of circulation for a while.'

'And you rose to fame while I was in hospital? Goodness me, life does go on, doesn't it?' She raised her delicate brows in mock surprise and he laughed again.

'Does the name Gideon Shale ring a bell?'

She shook her head. 'But it should?'

'Only if you happened to be one of my million readers.' He sighed mournfully and added, 'But obviously you're not.'

Eden's mouth curved into a teasing smile. 'I'm sorry. It must be awful to be famous and not be recognised by your own housekeeper!'

He nodded sadly. 'What is the world coming to?'

'Depressing!'

'Utterly!'

'Gideon Shale, eh?' She wrinkled her small straight nose. 'What made you choose that as a pseudonym?'

Joshua spread his hands in despair. 'She doesn't like it,' he groaned.

'Gideon Shale . . . Gideon Shale. Yes, I do like it. It's a good catchy name for an author.' Her eyes swept to the bookcase behind his table. Several blockbusters lined one of the shelves with Gideon Shale's name on the jackets. Memory stirred within her and she walked slowly around the table and took down one of the volumes, her fingers running lightly across the glossy red and black covers in which all of Gideon Shale's books were bound.

'This is your latest!' she exclaimed excitedly. 'Doc McKinley and just about everyone in the hospital was reading one of your books. Doc left this one on my bedside table but I must confess I didn't even open it.' Her grey eyes shone down on him. 'You *are* famous!'

'Whatever that means,' he growled and Eden knew instinctively her famous 'boss' was itching to get back to his writing. She placed the book back and came around to the front of the table and he wasted no time outlining her duties.

'First off you're never to touch anything on this table,' he warned, not altogether unpleasantly but Eden's cheeks flushed at his tone. 'The same goes for my bedroom. I keep notes in there and don't want anything disturbed.'

'What about your bed?' she asked. 'Should I make it?'

'No, I can do that. Best to stay out of there altogether.'

'I understand,' she murmured, hiding her relief. 'What about vacuuming and dusting?'

'Only when I'm not here. My work comes first. Anything else is unimportant. Above all, I'm not to be disturbed.'

Well she certainly had no intention of disturbing him, she thought indignantly. She would make certain she had as little to do with him as was humanly possible. Arrogant so-and-so!

'What about meals?' she asked, forcing a business-like tone into her voice. 'Shall we leave that up to me?'

Joshua picked up a pen and then immediately

let it drop. 'Yes,' he said irritably, 'anything will do, whatever you're capable of preparing.' He raised his black brows. 'Well? Anything else you care to discuss?'

'No, everything is perfectly clear, thank you.' She turned to march stiffly into the kitchen area where dishes were awaiting her.

'Oh, and Eden,' he called after her. 'I'm up at five every morning. I like to take a jog and a swim before breakfast.'

'Fine.' Why bother telling me, she thought. I don't care what you do in the wee hours of the morning.

But she did care. Each morning she awoke to the faint sound of his alarm clock as he got up for his early morning exercise. From her bedroom window she watched as he set off with Sam at his heels and she longed to join them. But she knew better than to invite herself along. If Joshua wanted her company he would have asked for it. Each morning as she served him breakfast she asked about his swim and if he had enjoyed his jog. Each time he heartily assured her that he had.

'It's the best time of the day,' he told her once. 'I work out any problems I'm having with my plot.'

'Oh!' she had answered, trying desperately to hide her disappointment for she realised it was the *privacy* he so treasured.

One evening as she said good night before retiring to her room, he looked up from his work. 'How would you like to join Sam and me tomorrow?' he asked casually. 'Think you could be up for five?'

She took her time in answering. The early hour wouldn't be a problem. She had watched him every morning since she had been here. But she didn't wish to intrude on his privacy. He enjoyed his jog and she knew he looked forward to it, setting off at a fast pace; a pace which she knew she was incapable of matching. Her legs just weren't strong enough and despite her exercises she still walked with a slight limp.

'Goodness me!' she answered brightly. 'I could never get up at *that* hour. Besides, I'm not much at jogging and I don't think anyone could force me into icy cold water so early in the morning.'

'Nonsense! You'll enjoy it.'

'No, I won't.'

'Of course you will. You're dying to go. I would have asked you sooner but I was having a particularly trying chapter and . . .'

'I'm *not* dying to go,' she broke in, cheeks crimson. 'Even if you had asked me sooner my answer would have been the same. I'm just not interested in jogging.'

'Just be ready at five,' he said flatly, returning to his work.

'I'm not going,' she insisted stoutly. 'It might be easy for you to manipulate people on the pages of your political thrillers but . . .'

'There's a clock on the top shelf over there which has an alarm,' he said as if she hadn't spoken. 'Take it and set it for a quarter to five. We leave sharply at five. As you know, I like to stick to a schedule.' He bent his head over his work considering the matter closed. She watched him for a few moments, resisting the urge to add anything further to their discussion. She had waited a long time for this invitation and now that he had invited her she almost wished he hadn't.

Almost! She was deliriously happy getting ready for bed that night. She set the little red alarm clock and placed it beside her bed and laid out the clothes she would wear. All during the night she kept a check on the time, fearful that the alarm wouldn't go off and that she would be left behind. Several times she was certain it had stopped and only after pressing it to her ear to listen to the steady beating for a few seconds did she place it back on the nightstand. Never had any night lasted so long.

When the first light of morning crept up to her windows Eden didn't see it. Nor did she hear the soft blurp of the old alarm clock as it hiccupped the arrival of a quarter to five. Awake most of the long night, Eden had finally slipped into an exhausted slumber.

At precisely five o'clock, the door to her bedroom burst open and Joshua stood glowering across at her sleeping form.

CHAPTER FOUR

'COME on, Eden, up!'

Her eyes flew open and she stared sleepily up at him before realisation of why he was here suddenly set in. She sat up, clutching the sheet to her chest.

'What time is it?' she asked, stifling a yawn.

'Time to be up,' he growled impatiently, lifting her from the bed and setting her on the floor. 'You overslept.'

'But I couldn't have,' she protested, trying to see past him to the little alarm clock. 'I haven't been to sleep and the alarm hasn't gone off.'

'The alarm went off almost twenty minutes ago and you were snoring when I came in.'

'Don't kid me, Joshua,' she said curtly, rubbing her arms against the cool morning air. 'I wouldn't know how to snore and that alarm hasn't gone off. You're being difficult, that's all, trying to make it look like I'm keeping you from your precious schedule.'

She glared up at him and he surprised her by smiling, a smile which was remarkably gentle under the circumstances.

'You're cold,' he said caringly, placing his huge hands on her shoulders and gently massaging them. Still half asleep she snuggled against him, his clean male scent extremely pleasant to her nostrils. Her cheek was pressed against his chest and he smoothed the wispy tendrils of hair away from the soft curve while she peeped up at him through the silky fringe of her lashes, eyes a deep smoky colour, the delicate skin underneath smudged with purple. He lowered his head and pressed his lips against them like an adult soothing away the hurts of a child. Eden stretched her arms around him, desperately needing someone to cling to and to hold her. His hands moved lightly down her back, setting her skin on fire. She trembled and he stood her away from him, his eyes roaming down her slender figure. The thin white cotton nightie revealed the almost child-like figure it was meant to conceal. With the direct sunlight behind her, every sweet curve was delicately portrayed. She raised a trembling hand and passed it through her hair, the movement extremely provocative in its innocence.

He was dressed in a navy blue track suit with white stripes running down the arms and legs. The jacket was zipped only part-way and she could see the silky black hairs against his brown chest. Her eyes swept up to his face, the wide cheek bones casting shadows along the contours of his cheeks while his green eyes flicked lazily over her, studying her from top to bottom! Eden folded her arms across her chest, suddenly self-conscious and he reached for her bathrobe and handed it to her and she gratefully accepted it, clutching it to her like a protective suit of armour, not daring to meet his eyes as she kept her own lowered.

'Do you still want me to go with you?' she asked, her voice filled with uncertainty as he helped her into the robe.

'Yes, even though you've managed to waste my time.' His smile took the sting from his words and caused her breath to catch in her throat. 'I'll leave you to get dressed,' he said, his hand cupping the

side of her face while he gave her the full impact of
those devilish green eyes. 'I've brought you a cup
of tea.' His hand dropped to the slender column of
her throat and her skin tingled against his touch.
'Drink it while you get ready. Sam and I will wait
for you out back.'

Eden watched him go and then sat on the edge
of her bed, her whole body trembling. The cup of
tea was on the nightstand and she reached for it
with both hands trying to keep it steady as she
sipped at it. She marvelled that she could still feel
the touch of his hands and she knew the gooseflesh
on her arms wasn't caused by the cold!

She dressed quickly into the clothes she had set
out the night before; comfortable faded jeans, a
rose coloured sweat shirt and with her one piece
bathing suit on underneath of a bluish green
colour.

Joshua and Sam were waiting for her at the
back of the cabin like he had promised. His green
eyes flicked over her, resting finally on her open-
toed sandals.

'You can't wear those. Don't you have any
joggers?'

'These will do. I wear them all the time.'

'Not where we're going, you can't.' He turned
and indicated with his arm. 'We're going through
that part of the wood. There's a path but it's
narrow and rough and in places overgrown with
scrub. You'll need something sturdy on your feet.'

She looked where he had indicated. It was a part
of his property she had never explored. Indeed, she
had often thought of it as a jungle and on her
walks with Sam had carefully avoided it, walking
instead through the cleared parts of the wood. She
turned back to him.

'There?' she asked weakly, wondering how she would ever manage on legs which were still causing her some difficulty while walking. 'But you never go there on your jogs.'

'It's not as bad as it looks,' he assured her without success. 'The path leads to a lagoon which is on my property. It's quiet and it's peaceful and very beautiful. I want to show it to you.'

Eden flushed with pleasure at this. It was like he was sharing something with her; something private and wonderful.

'Just a minute,' she said shyly. 'I've got some sand shoes.' She quickly returned to her bedroom and came back a few minutes later wearing a pair of pink sand shoes which Joshua eyed rather critically before turning to lead the way.

The path was narrow and it certainly was rough! It took every speck of her stamina to keep up as he led the way with Sam between them. It seemed to Eden they had trudged for hours before Joshua finally called a halt. Beads of perspiration clung to her top lip and her fine blonde hair clung damply to the sides of her pink-stained cheeks.

'We'll take a rest here,' Joshua said, taking her arm and leading her under the cooling shade of a huge flowering banksia tree. Eden sank gratefully on to the soft green grass growing under the shade of the tree and pressed her back against the trunk. She gazed up at the leathery looking leaves, bright yellow flowers standing erect in cylindrical spikes among the green. Around and beyond, several more banksias grew with blossoms of scarlet and rose and bright lemon yellow.

A movement caught her eye. Joshua pressed a finger to his lips, motioning her to be quiet. A gigantic bird, the size of an overgrown turkey, darted out of the brush and raced down the narrow, overgrown path. Its head was a vibrant bright red and there was a brilliant yellow ring at the base of its neck. The plumage was dark grey-brown, the legs sturdy with big, well-developed toes. Eden had never seen such a beautiful but strange looking bird.

'What was *that*?' she asked when the bird had disappeared into the banksia trees.

Joshua chuckled and stretched his long legs in front of him, his shoulder touching hers. 'That was a scrub turkey,' he told her. 'There are several around here and we're likely to see a few more before we get to the lagoon.'

'A *turkey*?' She looked inquisitively up at him. 'You mean they're turkeys which have gone wild?'

He shook his head. 'They're not even remotely related to the turkey we enjoy at Christmas. In fact their true name is "megapode" which is derived from two Greek words, *mega* meaning large, and *podos* meaning foot. You saw how strong its legs were and the size of its toes? That's because they're not very good fliers and prefer to run to safety rather than fly although they can manage to get themselves into trees and glide from one tree to another.' He smiled down at her upturned face. 'Now wasn't seeing that scrub turkey worth the trek along this twisting path?'

Eden nodded and turned away from him, disturbed by the closeness of his body and his shoulder touching her own, causing her heartbeats to quicken. She swallowed hard.

'Are they only found around here?' she asked in a faintly tremulous voice.

'They like banksia dominated forests along the Queensland coast,' he answered, his eyes on her delicate profile as she continued to watch where the turkey had disappeared. 'But they're mainly found in scrubs and humid rainforests. I have a friend in the Darling Downs who receives regular visits from a pair in his own back garden so they are fairly sociable and don't seem confined to any one area.'

They sat in companionable silence for several minutes with Sam stretched in front of them. Overhead, colourful birds darted and swooped between the branches of the trees while the sun filtered through the thick luxurious foliage forming lacy designs on the sweet smelling grass. Bees hummed as they sucked on the nectar of the fragrant flowering bushes. Cool sea breezes fanned their cheeks and ruffled the silky blonde tresses of one and the thick unruly mass of the other. Eden had never known such peace.

'Ready?' Joshua sprang to his feet and held out his hand to her. Eden reached for it, watching while his strong brown hand covered her own small one as he pulled her gently to her feet.

'I could easily spend the whole day here,' she murmured softly, conscious of the fact he was still holding her hand and that she had no desire to remove it from his grasp.

'Good!' He gave her hand a squeeze. 'I thought you would like this part of the wood. You can visit here with Sam while I'm writing.'

'But . . . we can come here again, can't we?' She licked her lips. 'I mean . . . this could be part of your . . . *our* early morning exercise routine.' She held her breath, waiting for his reply. There would be no pleasure visiting the wood without him.

'Yes, this could be part of our routine,' he replied softly, green eyes mocking as though he had read her mind. A long finger reached out and traced the side of her cheek, moving slowly down the slender throat. Eden shivered and he smiled. 'It's easy to see you've been a long time without a man's touch!' A hardness crept into his eyes. 'Did you love him?'

Eden blinked, puzzled. 'Who?'

He frowned. 'Your boyfriend, of course. The one who died in the accident. The one you can't seem to forget.'

Eden bit her lip and lowered her eyes. She should clear up about the accident, tell him about her family, but the wounds were still too raw, the pain too intense.

'Please!' she begged and he heard the desperation in her voice and saw the naked misery in her eyes. 'I can't talk about it. Don't . . . don't make me,' she added brokenly.

Joshua sucked in his breath. 'He must have been quite a guy!' He grabbed her shoulders, fingers digging cruelly into her soft flesh. 'He can't come back to you, Eden. Face up to it. He's gone! Dead!'

'Stop!' she cried out, tears filling her eyes. 'You don't understand. You never will!'

His hands slid down her arms. 'Forget him, Eden. Stop torturing yourself with memories. You're tearing yourself apart.' His green eyes were fiercely intent as they held her own. 'You want to forget him,' he said huskily. 'I can feel it. If I kissed you right now I could make you respond. If I made love to you it would be my name on your lips, not his!'

Fear clutched at her throat. 'You wouldn't dare!' she gasped, struggling to free herself, but his hands tightened on her arms as he drew her closer.

Words of protest stuck in her throat as those fierce green eyes rendered her incapable of uttering them.

'Oh, I would dare all right,' he taunted and even as he spoke Eden could feel her heart clamouring in her chest. His hands moved slowly to her back, his touch deliberately seductive as he pressed her slender body against his lean hardness. Physically she lacked the strength to free herself. Emotionally she was caught up in a whirlwind, her brain spinning crazily while every nerve in her body awakened and responded to his touch. She was completely in his power to do with as he wished.

But he didn't kiss her; he merely smiled and released her, leaving her trembling in front of him. 'Ah, yes,' he gloated, a sardonic smile twisting the handsome line of his mouth while triumph gleamed in the wicked green of his eyes. 'It would be easy all right but who wants to compete with a memory!'

Eden backed against the tree, hands pressed behind her. She felt as if he had slapped her, stunned not only by his words, but also by what had happened to her. She had never been with a man, had never had the desire. Boyfriends she had had plenty of and most had tried unsuccessfully to get her into their bed. They had eventually accepted her explanation that she didn't believe in casual affairs, that if she ever did sleep with a man it would be the one she knew she would eventually marry.

And now here she was with Joshua Saunders, alias Gideon Shale. Right from the beginning she had allowed him to manoeuvre her. She had cooked his meals and cleaned his cabin and she knew now she *loved* doing it! At night when she closed her eyes it was *his* face and not her family's whose vision wouldn't go away and which had a comforting and reassuring effect on her. His touch unnerved her and now she understood why. *She had fallen in love with him!* He only had to look at her and her heart did crazy things in her chest.

How could she have been so dumb not to guess what was happening to her; what he was doing to her. Surely she had suffered enough. To fall for a man like Joshua Saunders was like falling for the Devil himself. He could have no possible use for her. He was rich and famous and if that wasn't enough, he was also unbearably handsome. He had everything going for him while she had nothing at all.

Eden knew what she must do. Get herself as strong as she possibly could in the least amount of time and bid him farewell. To leave before he thought she was one hundred per cent fit would be unthinkable. He wouldn't allow it. He was also extremely domineering!

She smoothed back her hair and pushed away from the tree. 'Well, now that you've settled that for yourself,' she said smoothly, amazing herself by the calmness of her voice and gaining confidence from it, 'shall we proceed to the lagoon?'

He bowed slightly. 'After you, fair maiden.'

She hated walking in front of him. Never before had she been so conscious of her limp. Her steps were stilted more than usual and she knew it was because she was trying too hard to make herself walk smoothly and evenly. Joshua was only inches behind, another worrying factor because she knew it must be hard for him to shorten his naturally long stride to keep pace with her slow, awkward ones. She had looked forward to this outing, to be part of something he enjoyed. Now all she wanted was to prove to him that she was made of such strong fibre that he could never hope to have any control over her life.

Sam bounded ahead, happy to be on the move again and completely oblivious to the wretched thoughts of the young woman trailing behind.

'Careful, Eden.' Joshua's voice rumbled behind on a warning note. 'You're walking too fast! We're almost to the lagoon and there are some pretty sharp stones which manage to work their way through the soil. Keep your eyes on the path and for God's sake, slow down!'

Even as he issued the warning a stone caught Eden's shoe, twisting her foot. She cried out in alarm and would have fallen had Joshua's strong arms not grabbed and steadied her. Her fear of falling was so great she forgot about her earlier resolve to appear strong and efficient. She leaned against him, grateful for his support.

'Are you all right?' he asked as he knelt in front of her to examine the slender ankle. The sun shone on his hair, and she noticed the blue highlights, the sleek blackness giving way to blue-tipped wings. She longed to touch it, her fingertips tingling with the desire to do so, to feel the texture and the strength of that thick, luxurious mass. Instead she placed her hands on his shoulders to steady herself as he examined the foot which wasn't injured. The muscles of his broad shoulders throbbed under her palms as he expertly manipulated her ankle, thrilling her by his touch which seemed more like a caress.

There was really no point in telling him she wasn't injured. He could find that out for himself

while she rested by holding on to him which was
perfectly innocent under the circumstances, she
told herself rather happily.

'Not even sprained!' he said finally, standing up
and once again towering above her. His eyes were
dark and moody as they settled on her flushed
little face, grey eyes luminous from her inner
feelings.

'You sound disappointed!' she flared suddenly,
meeting his stormy glance.

'Don't be ridiculous!' he snarled. 'You were
walking too fast and I warned you about the path
being dangerous. You could have broken your
ankle. Perhaps that's what you were trying to do!'

'Are you crazy?' she sputtered. 'I've had enough
breaks to last a lifetime.' She flicked back her
blonde hair with trembling hands. The man was
insufferable, he really was. How could she possibly
love and hate him both at the same time? 'If I was
walking too fast it was to get away from *you*! You
were practically breathing down my neck! If I *had*
broken my ankle, it would have been *your* fault!'

Joshua shook his dark head in wonder. 'Female
logic never ceases to amaze me,' he returned
cynically. 'To spare myself further harassment I
had better carry you.' Before Eden realised what
was happening he had picked her up and swung
her unceremoniously over his broad shoulder. In
this highly undignified fashion she was transported
to the lagoon and set down none too gently on the
white powdery sand.

'How dare you treat me this way?' she hissed,
smoothing her rumpled sweat shirt and jeans. 'I'm
not a sack of potatoes to be carted and . . . and
dumped.'

'And had I known you were going to be so

much trouble,' he growled, 'I would have left you back at the cabin.'

'Why didn't you then? I wouldn't have minded.' She placed her hands on her hips. 'Just remember it was your idea that I come.'

'I usually have such *good* ideas,' he countered.

'But not this time?' she asked, feeling hurt and in the way.

He studied her in silence for a few seconds before shaking his head. 'Who knows? It worried me ... leaving you.' He glared down at her, dangerous lights appearing in his eyes. 'I'll have you know I mucked up a whole chapter on your account.'

'Isn't that just like a man!' she scoffed but feeling secretly pleased that he had worried about her, not that it had been necessary of course, but it was nice just the same. 'Blames the little woman for every mistake he makes.'

Suddenly he smiled, the dark expression lifting from his handsome features and replaced with devilish amusement. Eden regarded him with suspicion wondering what had caused this change of attitude.

'You're a regular little wildcat, do you know that?' he said and she got the feeling he had paid her a compliment.

Her suspicion mounted. 'What do you mean by *that*?' she asked, grey eyes glowering.

His easy chuckle washed over her, bringing even more colour to her flushed cheeks. 'Well, you've been through so much. And you're small, a gust of wind could blow you away yet...' His smile broadened and she knew he was enjoying himself at her expense. 'Yet you always come out fighting ... with words if not with blows.'

Eden opened her mouth to comment on that but quickly clamped her lips shut when she saw what he was doing. He was undressing himself! Already his track suit top lay on the sand and he was stepping out of the bottoms. Her cheeks flamed with colour as she quickly turned away. He was practically *naked*, the small black bathing suit barely concealing his masculinity!

She fumbled with her own top, fingers clumsy as she attempted to pull it over her head.

'Here, let me help,' he offered and before she had a chance to protest her sweat shirt lay on top of his track suit.

'I can do it,' she mumbled self-consciously, stepping well away from him while she slipped out of her jeans. In her one piece bathing suit she looked extremely over-dressed compared to his almost naked form. There wasn't an ounce of excess flesh on him, his whole body tanned, fit and muscular. She couldn't meet his eyes, his rugged masculinity unnerving her to such an extent that she became angry with herself.

He smiled down at her, teeth dazzling against the deep tan of his skin. 'Out of respect for you,' he drawled in a sexy voice which she guessed he was using to deliberately tease her, 'I decided to wear trunks. Ordinarily, I swim in the nude!'

'You could have spared yourself the trouble,' she said pointedly, boldly allowing her eyes to sweep the length of his body, passing quickly over the part of him barely concealed by the thin band of cloth. 'You don't need to parade your wares in front of me Joshua Saunders, because I've never been impressed by men who fancy themselves as peacocks!'

His appreciative roar of laughter thundered

around them, silencing the parrots, galahs and
rosellas perched high on the branches of the trees
circling the tranquil blue waters of the lagoon.
Eden dug her toes in the soft sand, feeling the
warm morning sun on her bare arms and
shoulders. Ignoring him, she walked stiffly to the
edge of the pool and taking a deep breath slowly
submerged into the refreshing coolness.

Her body felt weightless. The buoyancy of the
salt water kept her afloat and she swam effortlessly
with long, graceful strokes. Joshua stood on the
sand watching her, smiling at her obvious
enjoyment.

'Are you going to stand there posing all
morning, Mr Body Beautiful?' she called out. 'Or
are you going to join me in a swim?'

He did a shallow dive into the water, surfacing
beside her. His black hair gleamed and fell across
his wide brow, green eyes matching grey for
merriment.

'You're full of surprises,' he said with a happy
grin. 'I thought for sure I would have to drag you
kicking and squealing into the water.'

She had thought so too but there seemed no
need to confirm his suspicions. The water was
delightfully pleasant, not icy cold like she had
thought it might be. She swam away, putting a
comfortable distance between them. 'You mean
you *hoped* you would have to!' she yelled happily
back at him.

He swam after her. 'Keep away from me!' she
shrieked, her face brightly animated as she pushed
her wet hair out of her eyes. 'I don't trust you!
You might try ducking me or something silly like
that!'

'I wouldn't dream of doing such a thing,' he

returned, a malicious gleam dancing in the clear green of his eyes.

'Well, just remember you're used to this water and I'm not,' she reminded him. 'And you're much stronger than I am. If you ducked me I could easily drown!'

He heard the thin ribbon of fear in her voice and he smiled gently to reassure her. 'Try standing.'

'What?'

'Touch the bottom. The water should only be up to your shoulders. There's nothing to fear.'

Eden regarded him with great suspicion. Was *he* standing? The water was barely up to his waist but he could be fooling. Gingerly, cautiously, Eden straightened her legs. Her toes touched bottom. He was right. The water hardly reached her shoulders.

'I thought for sure it would be deep here,' she said, feeling foolish but at the same time enormously relieved.

'It's low tide,' he informed her softly. 'I can understand your fear though and you've every right to exercise caution around unfamiliar water.' He waved towards the mouth of the lagoon where the tide waters were pouring back to the ocean. 'At high tide the lagoon fills up and gets pretty deep. Well over your head so I advise you not to swim here on your own in the late afternoons,' he added on a final warning note.

Eden looked at the mouth of the lagoon and beyond where the waves were breaking. She hadn't ventured into the surf since the day she had watched the family which had seemed so much like her own and who had indirectly been responsible for her long trek down the beach where she was to meet Sam who led her to Joshua. She turned slowly back to Joshua and saw that he too was watching the pounding surf.

'You don't need to stay here to swim,' she told him quietly. 'I wouldn't mind if you went into the surf. The waves look great . . . perfect for body surfing.'

Joshua looked down at her and smiled. Her eyes were filled with apprehension and he knew she didn't want to be left alone nor could he take her into the wildly tossing waves where the outgoing tide could easily pick her up and ride her out to sea.

'No, it's nice here,' he answered casually and her eyes flooded with relief. His huge hands circled her waist and he lifted her in the air. Then he slowly lowered her until her face was level with his own. 'Do you know what I'm going to do?' he asked huskily.

Eden's heart caught in her throat. 'What?' she was barely able to whisper.

She could feel his warm breath fanning her cheeks and she was very much aware of his hard, muscular body against the softness of her own.

'Well, first of all I want to say thank you for all the work you've done around the cabin. The old place has never looked so nice.' His arms tightened around her, moulding her slender form to the masculine contours of his body. Eden's heart hammered crazily in her chest. She hardly heard the huskily spoken words as his hands worked their way down her body settling on the soft mounds of small, firm buttocks. She tried desperately to move away but her actions only served to caress him and she became instantly aware of his full arousal.

'Next, I'm going to kiss you!' One hand swept
up to her head as his mouth covered hers. The
kiss was gentle at first, almost featherlike upon
her trembling lips. Eden stiffened, then as the
pressure of his mouth increased, her body
awoke, every nerve and sense tingling as fire lit
her veins.

Her arms moved up to encircle his neck, fingers
moving lovingly through the hair she had so
longed to touch. She returned his kisses with a
passion she never knew herself capable of, thrilling
in the sheer ecstasy of just being in his arms.
Joshua cradled her against him and with her face
snuggled in his neck he carried her out of the water
and laid her down on his track suit. She gazed up
at him, grey eyes smoky with passion and with her
slender arms held lovingly out to him. He lay
beside her, once more gathering her close to him,
lips seeking hers and performing their miracle.

'You're beautiful, Eden,' he whispered against
her cheek, his lips nuzzling the shell-like structure
of one pink little ear. She clung to him, arms
stroking the broad expanse of his back, fingertips
touching the band of his swimming trunks. Joshua
groaned and covered her thigh with his, sensuous
mouth like liquid fire against her throat resting on
her throbbing pulse.

Eden's heart almost stopped beating when his
mouth sought her shoulder and then down to the
sweet curve of her breast. She arched towards him,
putty in his hands, her body begging for
fulfilment. He reached behind her, gently lifting
her to unfasten the snaps of her bathing suit,
pulling the top down to reveal the small rounded
breasts with their erected pink tips.

Sanity returned with a rush. Eden tugged

frantically at his dark head, pulling on his hair as he nuzzled her breasts.

'Stop!' she cried out, managing to get her hands between them and pushing at his chest. 'Stop this . . . this *madness*!'

Joshua moved slowly away from her, green eyes stormy and burning with a light she had never seen in them before; a light she had never seen in anything *human*! She shivered and pulled at her bathing suit, turning herself away from him as he sat silently observing her, that fierce light growing in intensity.

'*Madness?*' he uttered harshly. 'Is that how you saw it? Is that what it was to you? *Madness?*'

Eden grabbed her sweat shirt and held it in front of her. 'I'm not blaming you,' she said shakily. 'It was the setting,' she attempted to explain. 'It's so very beautiful here. The water is the same colour as the sky and the trees . . .'

He grabbed her arm forcing her to look at him. She shrank from the blazing anger in his eyes. 'Christ, woman! Have you no feelings? Do you think I'm made of stone? You were practically begging for me to make love to you and now you turn poetic on me saying it was the water and the sky and the trees!' He dropped her arm and sprang to his feet while she gazed helplessly up at him. She loved him so. Her heart was almost bursting with her feelings for him and she had loved his lovemaking and had longed to go further. But did he love her? No, *he hated her*! It was there . . . in his eyes, in his attitude. He had made love to her merely because she was *there*. If he loved her, truly loved her, he would have told her.

'I . . . enjoyed your lovemaking, Joshua,' she said rather primly, hoping to appease him. She gave a shaky little laugh. 'It . . .' She swallowed hard, her eyes still on his, wondering why he should look so incredulous when she was only trying to ease his injured pride. 'It was very nice.'

'*Nice!*' he exploded. 'Nice? Are you nuts or is it me who has gone crazy?' He held up his hand. 'Don't bother answering that, please. I'm the fool, all right. It's your lover, isn't it,' he stated matter-of-factly. 'You can't get over him.'

Eden squeezed her eyes shut and bowed her head while tears pricked painfully beneath her lids. Joshua grabbed her hands and pulled her to her feet. She forced herself to look at him. His face was dark with rage.

'Well?' he rasped. 'Aren't you going to say something? Aren't you going to deny it?'

'I have nothing to say to you, Joshua Saunders,' she said in a surprisingly chilly voice. She wrenched her hands free. 'Nothing at all!'

CHAPTER FIVE

'WHAT are you doing?'

Eden whirled to find Joshua standing behind her at the kitchen sink. It was the longest sentence either had spoken since their passionate kisses at the lagoon over a week ago. Each had gone about their duties hardly sparing the other a glance, the only spoken words being the odd 'please' or 'thank you' while sharing meals. Eden had accompanied him on the early morning jogs and swim and while he had showered and shaved she had prepared the enormous breakfasts her appetite now demanded she consume.

But they were like strangers sharing the same meals and sleeping under the one roof, careful not to touch the other in passing or engaging in any real conversation. To each it was like the other didn't exist. At least that's what they pretended.

'What does it look like I'm doing?' Eden asked flippantly, unscrewing the cap from a bottle of tablets and filling a glass with water.

He snatched the bottle from her hand and read the label. 'What are these things?' he demanded harshly.

Eden tilted her head. 'Tranquillisers.'

'Tranquillisers?' he exploded, his green eyes searching her face. 'What do you need these for?'

She reached for the bottle of tablets but he held them well out of her reach.

'Hand over my property.'

His eyes were filled with disgust. 'You don't

need this stuff!' His eyes trailed over her body. She was wearing white shorts and a sleeveless sun shirt and her pale blonde hair was still slightly damp from their swim. Her ever increasing appetite had put on some of the extra weight she so desperately needed and the sun had tanned her skin to a lovely honey colour. Even her limp had all but disappeared.

'I do,' she said, desperation creeping into her voice. 'Doc McKinley said I was to take four a day. They're muscle relaxants.' Again she reached for the bottle and then watched in horror as he tipped the tablets down the sink, washing them down the drain with water.

'What else have you got?' he demanded, grabbing her arm and drawing her close to him. 'I'm not having you turn into a junkie!'

She stared up at him, her eyes blazing with contempt. 'How dare you do this to me. You're not a doctor. Doc McKinley says . . .'

'I don't give a damn what Doc McKinley says,' he rasped angrily. 'Now answer me, Eden. What else have you got stashed away?'

She pressed her lips shut refusing to answer.

'All right, have it your way.' He released her and she watched while he went through the kitchen cupboard knowing he would find nothing there.

'Satisfied?' she gloated when his search finally came to a fruitless end.

'There's still the bathroom and your bedroom,' he remarked casually and she trailed after him down the short hallway. The bathroom revealed nothing and again she smirked with satisfaction.

He went to her bedroom and flung open the door. She raced ahead of him hardly believing that he would actually rifle through her personal belongings.

'Don't think I'm going to permit you to go through my drawers!' she flared, colour staining her cheeks. 'After all, I'm not allowed to touch even a pen of yours!'

'Out of my way, Eden,' he said as she placed herself in front of her bureau, her arms spread protectively across its width.

'Get out of my room. You have no business here.'

'This isn't your room, it's mine. I'm merely lending it to you until such time as you get better and can fend safely for yourself. Now if you don't get away from that bureau I'll drag you from it.'

'Oh, all right,' she mumbled and turning swiftly opened the top drawer and withdrew a bottle of a well-known commercial brand of vitamin capsules. He took the bottle and examined the contents as though expecting to find something other than the vitamins mixed in with the capsules. Apparently satisfied he handed the bottle back to her and she quickly returned them to the drawer shutting it and again facing him, her grey eyes gleaming with triumph.

But he wasn't to be convinced so easily. He pushed her aside and opened the drawer she had just closed. 'What are these?' he asked, holding up a much smaller bottle. He unscrewed the cap and emptied several tablets into his hand. His green eyes glittered dangerously down at her and she knew she had lost the battle.

'They're sleeping tablets,' she sighed wearily, crossing the room to flop on to her bed. 'If you destroy those I won't get any sleep.'

He studied her for several long moments and

she got the feeling his eyes were microscopes penetrating into her very soul, dissecting every nerve and sinew in her body.

'*Why* won't you get any sleep?' he asked at length, his long frame leaning against her bureau, feet crossed at the ankles and her precious bottle of tablets dangling carelessly from his fingers. 'You're up every morning at five, you hike in the woods for a mile, you swim for at least an hour and then you jog along the beach. You prepare three meals a day, you play with Sam and you've even started a garden. I've watched you, Eden. By seven o'clock at night you're yawning and can barely keep your eyes open but even so you sit up for an extra two hours and read. How could you possibly need sleeping tablets?'

She hunched miserably away from him, unable to meet those all-knowing eyes. 'Because .. if I don't take them, I'll have nightmares,' she answered in a small voice.

He placed the tablets on the top of her bureau and went over to sit beside her. He reached for her hands and held them between his own. 'Tell me about your nightmares,' he said quietly.

'N-no!' she answered in a quivering voice. 'I can't. I just can't!'

His grip tightened on her hands and she could feel his enormous strength. It was like he was offering her a lifeline and she knew she had no other choice but to accept it. She took a deep breath and turned to face him, her eyes never leaving his as she related her tragic story.

'It wasn't a lover that died in the accident,' she told him, her eyes filled with grief. 'It was my family ... my whole family, my parents and my twin sisters. It was the girls' sixteenth birthday and

Dad had just bought a new car. Mother had taken the championship at a golf tournament and I had just received news I had taken top marks in my mid-term exams.'

A sad, wistful smile touched her lips. 'We all had something to celebrate and so Dad booked us in at Melbourne's newest and most exclusive restaurant. It was such a happy evening, we had such fun . . .' She was holding tightly on to his hands, her eyes still locked to his finding the courage there to continue on. 'It had started to rain, just a fine drizzle really but it was enough to make the road slippery. There was an articulated lorry and . . . and we were singing silly little songs like *She'll be coming around the mountain* and then the next thing we knew we were hurtling over the embankment and there were screams, dreadful screams. That's all I remember. I woke up in hospital and to,' she cleared her throat and gulped, unaware that tears were streaming down her cheeks, 'and to the knowledge that I no longer had a family.'

He held her for a long time, rocking her gently in his arms, his hands soothing the damp strands of hair from her cheeks. She tasted the salt from her own tears when his mouth pressed against hers and his cheeks were damp from the steady flow which he knew had welled up inside her for far too long and which now were finally cleansing the wounds which had been allowed to grow and fester. He murmured soft words against her ears, his hands stroking and caressing her body, soothing her the way one would a hurt and injured animal. Finally her sobs subsided and gradually she became still in his arms. He pulled back her covers and put her in bed and she was too

exhausted to utter a word as he drew the curtains
and left her to sleep, the bottle of sleeping tablets
in his hand which she knew he would dispose of.
Her eyes closed and her body felt very heavy. She
knew she would have no further need for sleeping
pills and she also knew she would no longer suffer
her terrible nightmares. Joshua Saunders had done
what no doctor could. He had given her back her
life!

During the days which followed Eden talked
constantly about her family, telling Joshua
everything she remembered starting from the time
the twins were born and how she had spent hours
watching them sleep and eat and gurgle and play.
She told him about their family picnics and their
holidays in the mountains and how her father had
taught them all to ski. She baked him her mother's
favourite recipes and amused him with funny little
happenings which occur in families and are only
shared with the one you love.

And she loved Joshua. Her love grew deeper for
him with each passing day and she could feel it
growing second by second. She watched him while
he worked at his desk, loving the way his black,
unruly hair fell over his forehead. She marvelled at
how quickly his long, brown fingers skimmed over
the typewriter keys and she read each of his books
with glowing pride.

He would look up from his work and find her
eyes on him and smile across at her. During these
times she would wish he would make some
indication that he wanted her beside him, that he
wanted to make love to her. Her body ached for
him with a desire which tormented her and which
she wasn't ashamed of. At night in her bed she
would strain her ears listening to his movements,

worrying that he was staying up too late, working too hard.

Her restlessness increased. After lunch she and Sam started taking long walks in the wood. On one such occasion they came across a young man sketching a scrub turkey in the banksia trees. Eden watched the young artist and when the sketch was completed walked up to him.

'That's very good,' she commented honestly. The young man swung around, his blue eyes guilty. He was dressed only in a pair of faded old jeans and he was blond with a scraggly blond beard. 'Do you often come here?' Eden enquired casually, wondering why the young man should look so guilty. 'It's a good place for sketching.' She smiled. 'By the way, I'm Eden Baines.'

The young man stood up, the sketch in his hand. 'I'm Bob Hastings,' he smiled back, holding the sketch out to her. 'You can have this if you like.'

Eden's eyes widened in surprise. 'Are you sure? I mean, don't you want to keep it for yourself?'

'No, I've got plenty. Besides, it isn't often a beautiful young girl comes skipping out of the woods to admire my work.' His grin was bright and Eden hid her smile. He couldn't be more than her age and far too cocky.

'Well, thank you very much,' she said, looking once more at the sketch. I shall treasure it always,' she added dramatically for his benefit.

'If you care to sit under that tree with the dog, I'll do a sketch of you both.'

'Really? Hey, Sam.' Eden patted the dog's majestic head. 'That sounds pretty good to me, how about you?'

Sam looked suitably bored and Eden and Bob

laughed. 'Which tree?' she asked. 'That one with the purple blossoms?'

'Yes, with your blonde hair and colouring it will be truly superb.'

Eden and Sam sat for their portrait. When it was finished and he had shown it to her, Eden could hardly believe hr eyes. This kid had talent!

'Where did you learn to sketch so well?' she asked, her voice and eyes filled with praise and enthusiasm.

'I didn't learn it, it's just something I've always enjoyed doing.'

'Well, I think if you put yourself under the guidance of a good instructor you could end up being famous.'

'Really?' The young man's eyes danced with pleasure.

'Yes, really,' she laughed, enjoying this pleasant conversation which made no demands on her. 'Do you live around here?'

'No, I'm from Brisbane. Me and a couple of mates have pitched camp near a lagoon just over the ridge from here.'

'A lagoon?' Eden asked weakly. It had to be Joshua's lagoon and knowing him the way she did she knew he wouldn't approve of anyone pitching camp on his property. 'You mean *that* lagoon just over there?' she asked, indicating with her arm. Perhaps there were other lagoons nearby. After all, she and Joshua had swum in his lagoon that morning and they certainly hadn't seen any campers.

'Yes, that one. We only just got here but when I saw a scrub turkey race by I had to sketch it. Lucky I did too otherwise we wouldn't have met.'

Eden shifted uneasily. 'Did you realise this is

private property?' she enquired. 'I happen to know the owner and I think it only fair to warn you that he wouldn't be at all pleased to learn that people are camping by the lagoon.'

The young man grinned. 'Sure, we saw the sign.' His voice became gruff: '"No Trespassing" it said but what harm can a few blokes do?'

'That's not up to either of us to decide,' Eden said quietly. 'If there's a "No Trespassing" sign you shouldn't have ventured on to this property.'

The young man's face hardened and suddenly Eden disliked him. His boyish charm had been a ploy and she had fallen for it. Now she saw the real stuff that Bob Hastings was made of.

'Well, seeing as how you claim to know the owner then perhaps you can put in a good word for us. We'll only be here for a couple of days and then we'll be off. We promise to leave everything neat and tidy and not a grain of sand will be disturbed.'

Eden sighed. 'All right,' she agreed. 'I'll see what I can do.'

She had meant to tell Joshua about the young man as soon as she got back to the cabin but when she arrived he was deeply engrossed in his work and she knew she had better wait for a more suitable time to inform him about the campers. She put the sketches on the breakfast bar while she busied herself preparing their evening meal.

When Eden had first started preparing their meals she did so with very little interest, hardly caring what she put on the table. But now every meal was carefully planned and expertly prepared. Tonight it was to be chicken and dumplings with tender sweet baby carrots from her own vegetable garden along with some freshly picked peas. For dessert fresh fruit salad made up from the many fruit trees which grew around the property, pawpaw, mangoes, and some avocados. And always a salad, tender lettuce leaves, slices of capsicum, cherry tomatoes, cheese diced and slivers of zucchini, lightly tossed with a dressing of oil and lemon with a smidgeon of garlic.

Joshua entered the kitchen area and sniffed appreciatively, placing his newspaper on top of the sketches without a glance. His eyes were on Eden as he watched her moving happily about the kitchen putting the final touches to their meal while at the same time arranging flowers in a bowl which he knew would be their centre-piece.

'Hey, kid,' he called out to her, a mischievous gleam in his eyes. 'Are you the same little waif who appeared on my doorstep one day a thousand years ago?'

She chuckled happily, smoothing her tanned hands against the apron tied around her slender waist. 'No, that wasn't me,' she replied impishly. 'That was merely my shadow.'

'Shadows of Eden,' he drawled, going over to her and tilting her chin to look into her eyes. 'What substance you turned out to be.'

Kiss me, she thought. You can read my mind, so please read it now! His green eyes darkened as he looked into her face, at the softly trembling mouth, the bloom in her cheeks. His hands slipped to her shoulders, his fingers kneading the soft flesh and then abruptly he released her, turning his attention to the salad she had just prepared.

'Mmm, that looks good,' he remarked, picking up a piece of the diced cheese and popping it into his mouth.

'Wait until you taste the chicken,' she told him,

forcing a brightness into her voice to hide the hurt and bewilderment she always felt when he turned away from her.

They took their time with the meal, chatting casually like old friends. There were occasions when Eden could have brought up the campers at the lagoon but she didn't want to say anything which could put a damper on his good spirits. Besides, mealtimes were truly the only occasions when she had him completely to herself and these times were very precious to her. She decided she would tell him in the morning while they went for their hike in the woods.

'I have to take a drive into Noosa tomorrow morning,' Joshua remarked as he helped himself to a second helping of dessert. 'How about coming with me this time?'

Before when he had invited her to go with him, she had always declined, not wishing to be the object of people's stares as she limped along the streets. Now she could think of nothing nicer than going with him, sitting beside him in the old truck and walking next to him along the footpaths.

'Why, I would love to,' she agreed happily, her grey eyes shining across at him. At his amused and slightly surprised expression she quickly added, 'I'm practically out of those seeds you got me and our larder is getting pretty thin. We'll need to do some grocery shopping.'

'Good. Make up a list and we'll leave right after breakfast. We'll skip your exercise tomorrow morning.' His eyes gleamed at her. 'I'll let you sleep until seven!'

The next morning Eden was up at her usual time preparing herself for her trip into Noosa. She washed her hair and brushed it until it shone with

a million lights. She tried on practically everything
in her wardrobe but nothing seemed to suit.
Nothing seemed to fit and everything appeared
drab and old. Finally she settled on a pale blue
skirt which was the best of the lot and topped it
with a white sleeveless blouse. Her white sandals
were from last summer and no longer in style. One
of her aunts, she couldn't even remember which
one, had gone to her home and selected the
clothing she needed for this trip to Queensland
and while the selection hadn't mattered to Eden at
the time, it certainly did now. She was in desperate
need for a whole new wardrobe. The wage Joshua
had dutifully given her each week in return for her
housekeeping was sitting untouched on the top of
her bureau. She took it and slipped it into her
shoulder bag. Eden Baines was going on a
shopping spree!

Breakfast was waiting for Joshua when he
appeared in the kitchen clad only in a black silk
robe. Eden had long since discovered that he
wasn't in the habit of wearing pyjamas because
none had ever appeared in the wash. He hadn't
shaved and the bluish-black stubble on his cheeks
and chin only added to his raw, seductive
masculinity. His robe was loosely tied at the waist,
exposing the broad wall of his chest and the silky
black hairs which covered it. As he walked
towards the breakfast bar, the strong brown
columns of his legs covered with the same silky
black hairs were exposed to her and what little the
robe did cover was etched clearly in Eden's
memory!

He was surprised that she was already up and
dressed. He glanced at the watch strapped to his
wrist. 'It's barely seven o'clock. I was going to

cook *you* breakfast this morning.' He looked at the
huge platter piled with ham and eggs and browned
potatoes and the pitcher of freshly squeezed juice
standing beside it. 'Although I doubt it would
have been as tempting as this.' He sat down and
served them both. 'I wonder if this is what married
life would be all about,' he drawled casually. 'At
any rate it's safe to assume that one day you will
make some man extremely happy.'

Eden found it difficult to swallow her food. 'Do
you . . . do you think you will ever marry?' she
asked innocently, buttering a slice of toast.

'I doubt it.' He looked across at her busily
buttering her toast. 'I would like to have a few
kids though. How about you?'

'Yes, I love children.' She nibbled at her toast.
She had put too much butter on it. 'But I would
never marry only for the sake of having children.'

'No, you would have to be desperately in love
with the man. You would make a good wife and a
good mother. Everything points to it.'

'I think you would make a good husband and
father,' she said, returning the compliment.

He chuckled. 'We sound perfect, don't we?
Perhaps we should get married!'

Eden's heart was pounding so loudly she felt
certain he must hear it. She returned his chuckle,
treating the matter as a joke the way he obviously
was. 'Oh, but you probably snore and you are in
the habit of appearing for breakfast each morning
before you shave.'

'Too true.' He let out a mournful sigh. 'And
you're so thin you would probably cut me to
shreds each time you rolled over at night.'

'Alas!' She pretended to groan. 'Neither of us is
perfect after all.' She folded her arms across the

table. 'How *dare* you say I'm thin. I'll have you
know I've put on at least ten pounds since I've
been here!'

'And in all the right places, too!' His green eyes
swept over her, bringing a rosy hue to her cheeks.
'Ten more pounds of perfect womanhood!'

He helped her tidy up the kitchen and then went
off to shave and shower appearing a half hour
later dressed in a pair of beige shorts and a
chocolate brown open-necked golf shirt. His hair
was still damp from his shower and swept neatly
to one side. After first ensuring there was plenty of
water available for Sam while they were gone, they
finally hopped into the truck and drove into
Noosa. The blue waters of the Pacific ocean, with
its white sandy beaches, stretched alongside them,
while overhead a bright sun shone in a cloudless
blue sky. The windows of the truck were open and
the soft sea breezes swept around them tossing
their hair.

Noosa was a bustle of activity, its sun-swept
beaches and modern shops enticing tourists from
far and wide. Shoppers crammed the streets, their
richly tanned bodies clad mainly in swimming
gear, bikinis on the young and not so very young
women, while men and boys wore mostly
swimming trunks or shorts. There was a gaiety and
casualness to the atmosphere which blended in
with Eden's feeling of well-being. Flowering
shrubs and swaying palms lined the main
thoroughfare which ran parallel to the ocean.
Sidewalk cafés dotted the street with brightly
coloured sun umbrellas protecting patrons from
the brilliant sun.

Joshua parked the truck in a shaded spot under
a flowering tulip tree with bright coral blossoms.

'I'll be busy getting some writing supplies,' he told her, 'so while I'm doing that why don't you have a look at the shops. We can buy the groceries later.'

'Fine,' she agreed smilingly. 'Shall we meet back here?'

He glanced at his watch. 'Yes, let's say in a couple of hours. Will that give you enough time?'

'Plenty.'

It was great fun browsing through the many shops all equipped with the latest gear. In Melbourne she knew the shops would still be selling winter wear but here in the land of eternal sunshine everything was designed for summer.

She loved the bright colours, the simple but alluring styles and with the extra weight she had managed to gain everything she tried on seemed just perfect. She bought two bikinis, one a bright lavender colour which deepened the grey of her eyes and the other a black which highlighted her blonde hair and golden tan. Her one piece bathing suit hadn't allowed her midriff to receive any tan but within a few days she knew this would be taken care of.

At another boutique she found some shorts and tops and at still another a few simple frocks which made her slender figure appear interesting and provocative. A straw sun hat and three pairs of sandals, each a different colour, completed her new wardrobe. There was still one more thing to do. She entered a beauty parlour and had her hair trimmed and shaped into a becoming new style. Enormously pleased with the results she soon found herself at a chemists shop and with the last of her money purchased some make-up.

Joshua was waiting for her when she appeared at the truck. His eyes widened in surprise when he

saw her, for she was wearing one of her new
frocks, her old clothes stuffed into one of her
parcels and she had applied some of the make-up
in one of the shops' ladies' rooms. Her blonde hair
curved becomingly around her cheeks and her eyes
sparkled with happiness.

'Hi,' she greeted him, feeling suddenly self-
conscious as his eyes swept over her from head to
toe. 'I hope I'm not late?' she asked a trifle
breathlessly, knowing full well she was almost a
half hour over the time he had allowed her.

'You are late but it was well worth it! You look
radiant. What have you done to yourself?' he
asked as he took her bundles from her and put
them in the truck.

'Oh, I just got a few things I needed,' she offered
casually, enormously pleased at his compliment.
'Did I really look so awful before?' she added
anxiously as an afterthought.

'Only like something the cat dragged in but in
your case, something Sam dragged in!' His green
eyes sparkled down at her and she laughed at his
good-natured teasing.

'With all my new finery,' she said, smoothing
the bright multi-coloured frock with her hands, 'I
hardly feel like grocery shopping. Couldn't we go
somewhere nice and have lunch first?'

'I'm one step ahead of you,' he smiled, locking the
doors of the truck and putting the keys in his
pocket. Taking her hand he led her down the street.
'I've booked us into one of my favourite restaurants where seafood is the speciality.' He winked
down at her upturned face. 'There's even a bottle
of champagne being chilled especially for us.'

The restaurant was located on the foreshore
overlooking the ocean. Joshua was received like

royalty and because Eden was his companion she
was given the same treatment. Their table was
located on a small balcony completely enclosed for
total privacy. Below them was the beach and Eden
could see the topless bathers which she had
become accustomed to on the stretch of beach in
front of Joshua's cabin. At first she had been
amazed by this custom but Joshua had informed
her that Noosa was famous for its topless bathers.
Now she barely noticed these sun-worshippers and
even admired their total lack of self-consciousness.
She thought of her new bikinis and decided that
she would do the same at the privacy of the lagoon
and then her eyes clouded when she remembered
the campers. She would have to inform Joshua but
not now. This occasion belonged to the two of
them and she didn't want to spoil it in any way.

Eden studied the menu with its dazzling
assortment of dishes but Joshua didn't even glance
at his. She looked up at him. 'What are you
having?' she asked.

'Lobster.'

'I'll have the same with lemon butter.' She gave
a light-hearted laugh. 'I like to dip the chunks into
it with my fingers. Would that disgust you?'

He shook his head. 'Nothing you do would
disgust me.' And she quickly lowered her eyes
because he had sounded so serious while she had
been only teasing.

Their orders were taken and the champagne was
served. The setting, the meal, the champagne and
the company was truly superb and more than once
Eden found it hard to believe that it actually was
herself sitting here, laughing and chatting and
looking dreamily into Joshua's long lashed, sexy
green eyes.

'You know everything about me,' she told him when they had finished their peach melbas, 'and I know so little about you. You've guided me through the worst part of my life and I dread the moment when I have to return to Melbourne.' She reached across the table and placed her hand on top of his. 'Tell me about yourself so I can remember it all when I no longer have you beside me.'

'I think I've plied you with too much champagne!' he drawled, his green eyes dark with some hidden meaning. He looked down at her hand and covered it with his own. Shivers of delight whisked up Eden's arm and trailed across to her heart.

'No, please,' she begged, her eyes pleading with him. 'Tell me about your family and all about you. How many brothers and sisters have you? Who do you look like? Your mother or your father?'

He removed his hand from hers and leaned back in his chair, his eyes hooded through lowered lids. 'I'm an only child,' he said flatly. 'My mother died from an overdose of sleeping pills when I was two years old and my father drank himself to death! An aunt raised me and put me through university where I managed to take out a degree in journalism. After that I covered political stories in countries ravished by war and where babies died from malnutrition while their mothers suckled them on breasts which had long gone dry. I returned to Noosa, bought the cabin, built a few complexes and now I'm endeavouring to write a few books.' He spread his hands wide. 'End of story.'

Eden stared at him, shocked. 'Is that the truth?' she asked in barely audible tones.

'Yup! Not a very pretty picture is it,' he answered tonelessly.

Compared to his life, Eden's had been heaven. She could hardly believe this warm, caring person had had such a dreadful life. No wonder he had felt no pity for her. No wonder he had been so angry about her tablets. She felt ashamed of herself and she told him so.

'I met an old-timer once,' he said in answer, 'and he told me that if everyone had a chance to toss their problems into a basket and take out someone else's they would be only too glad to have their own problems back!' He smiled across at her, his eyes gentle but now that she knew this new aspect of him, she saw they were tinged with sorrow. 'Life isn't easy, Eden, but it doesn't have to be hard either. Not if you have the courage to meet it head on!'

CHAPTER SIX

'DID we really buy all this?' Eden asked disbelievingly.

The groceries were spread across the small table and over the breakfast bar. 'We did,' Joshua stated, his eyes skimming with the same disbelief over the dazzling array.

'We had too much champagne,' Eden concluded, her grey eyes dancing with mischief. 'There's enough here to feed an army . . . two armies!' She looked at Joshua's tall, masculine form. 'I trust you are going to help me put all this away? After all, most of what we bought, you selected.'

'Of course I'll help.' He picked up a tin of sardines. 'Surely I didn't choose these?'

Eden laughed. 'You did, three tins as a matter of fact. Why, don't you like them?'

He shuddered. 'Give them to Sam unless you care for them. I can't bear even the smell of the things.'

'Oh dear.' She gave an exaggerated sigh. 'And here I was planning to make a casserole for tonight's dinner. Sardine *à-la-mode*!' She picked up one of the tins. 'I'll make Sam and I some sandwiches with them. Does Sam care for chilli do you think?'

'Chilli?' His eyes widened in horror. 'In sardines?'

'Uh, huh!' She smacked her lips. 'Truly delicious.'

He glanced over a broad shoulder at Sam sitting

in the doorway of the kitchen. 'Poor beast,' he muttered, walking over to give him a sympathetic pat. He straightened and looked again at the groceries. 'Let's just put away the perishables and go for a swim. We can put the rest away later.'

'I'm all for that,' Eden agreed, picking up a huge container of ice-cream and placing it in the freezer. 'Hand me the frozen goods,' she said, 'and we can pretend we're an assembly line.'

With the frozen goods put away, other perishables were safely stacked in the refrigerator leaving only toiletries, washing powders and the like. Eden took one of the bags her shopping was in and pulled out her two new bikinis.

'Look what I bought,' she said, holding them out to him. 'Do you like them?'

His black brows arched mockingly. 'May I reserve my decision until I see them on you?'

'You'll be stunned,' she teased. 'Ever hear of Marilyn Monroe?'

His dazzling smile cut straight to her heart. 'And you look better than *that*?'

'No comparison! It's just a good thing I don't live in Hollywood. I'd have to beat the agents off with a stick!'

But when she returned a few minutes later she was wearing her old one piece bathing suit. He had changed into his 'ribbon', as she liked to refer to his swimming trunks.

'What happened to Marilyn Monroe?' he asked.

'She changed her mind.'

'I see!' Colour seared her cheeks as he looked pointedly at her breasts. 'Perhaps she exercised more than you.'

'It's not that at all,' she huffed.

'What then? Inhibited by modesty?'

'Well, modesty *is* a virtue after all.'

'Why did you buy them if you were too shy to wear them?'

'I'm not shy. It's just that I need to tan my white spots.'

'Well, you're certainly not going to be able to accomplish that in that thing.'

'*Thing?*' She looked down at her suit. 'I'll have you know this "thing" cost a lot of money. And anyway, the way you people go around half nude I don't know if I'm quite ready for such ... well, exposure,' she said primly.

His green eyes mocked her. 'Surely you have bikinis in Melbourne?'

'Of course we do but at least they still *look* like bathing suits! The ones here are so ... are so *bare!*'

'Come on,' he chuckled, taking her hand. 'I'll respect your modesty today but tomorrow I fully expect you to wear a bikini, even,' and his eyes gleamed down at her, 'if I have to dress you myself.'

He led her towards the back door which meant they would be going through the woods to the lagoon and at the lagoon the campers were still most likely there.

'Let's not go to the lagoon,' she said, looking appealingly up at him. 'I think I would like to try the surf today.'

'Fine with me,' he agreed amicably. 'It's late anyway so the surf is the wiser choice.'

He held her hand all the way to the beach, their arms swinging between them. They had brought towels and Joshua spread them out and then taking her hand once more raced with her to the water. They plunged in together, surfacing with happy grins. 'Isn't this great?' she called out to him above the roar of the pounding waves. 'I'm

Win "Instantly" right now in another way

...try our *Preview Service*

Get 4 FREE full-length Harlequin Romance books

Plus
this handy,
compact umbrella
(a $10.00 retail value alone)

Plus a surprise
free gift

Plus lots more!

Our love stories are popular everywhere...and WE'RE CELE-BRATING with free birthday prizes—free gifts—and a fabulous no-strings offer.

Simply try our Preview Service. With your trial, you get SNEAK PREVIEW RIGHTS to six new HARLEQUIN ROMANCE novels a month—months before they are in stores—with 15%-OFF retail on any books you keep (just $1.66 each)—and Free Home Delivery besides.

THERE IS NO CATCH. You're not required to buy a single book, ever. You may even cancel Preview Service privileges anytime, if you want. The free gifts are yours anyway, as tokens of our appreciation.

It's a super sweet deal if ever there was one. Try us and see.

EXTRA! Sign up now-—automatically qualify to WIN THIS AND ALL 1986 "Super Celebration" PRIZE & PRIZE FEATURES...or watch for new prizes and new prize features NEXT MONTH at your favorite store.

glad you've had today off. You deserved a break.'

'And so did you,' he laughed, swimming with easy strokes to her side. 'Seeing as how you didn't give me a chance to cook breakfast, I'll prepare dinner tonight.'

'Really? I'll be getting spoilt,' she warned with a happy laugh. 'I might come to expect lunch in Noosa every day and then having my dinner served to me at night.'

'Who said anything about "serving"? I'm merely preparing!'

'And here I was picturing myself curled up in the lounge chair while you set a little tray across my knees, with a long-stemmed rose.' She pursed her lips, 'A yellow one, I think ... set in the middle of the tray with that crystal vase you have, you know the one, it has a chip at the top and a yellow napkin on the side to wipe away those delicious crumbs of some exotic dish ...'

He placed a large hand on top of her head and ducked her, effectively silencing her. When she surfaced she was coughing and spluttering and he gathered her into his arms.

'I told you I hated being ducked,' she lashed out at him, her happy mood drowned by the waves. 'You're nothing but a bully and ...'

This time he kissed her but she offered no protest.

'Kiss me again,' she husked, her arms creeping around his neck, her body thrillingly aware of his long lean length.

'If I kiss you again you know what will happen.' And his eyes were as turbulent as the seas pounding around them.

'Yes,' she whispered unashamedly. 'Oh, yes, Joshua.'

He picked her up and carried her out of the water, standing her on the towel. With one easy movement he wrapped the towel around her and carried her back to the cabin. 'Get dressed,' he ordered her tightly, 'while I make some dinner.'

Stunned by his sudden change of mood and the coldness in his eyes, Eden could only stand there, hurt and bewilderment showing clearly in her eyes. 'What's wrong?' she asked, in a tight voice. 'You kissed me and you've kissed me before. Why behave as though I committed some terrible crime by returning your kisses?'

Silence stretched like an eternal band between them. Finally Joshua spoke. 'Things are getting out of hand here and I mean to put a stop to it before it gets out of control.' He gave her a long, hard look. 'Affairs I can handle but I very much doubt if you could. You're the type of woman who expects marriage after a few romps in the hay, figuratively speaking.'

'I can't believe you're saying this to me,' she returned, trying desperately to keep her voice steady. 'I'm not a child although you probably see me as one merely because when we first met I was extremely vulnerable.' She straightened to her full height. 'I fully expect to enter into a few affairs before I settle down,' she said unconvincingly. 'I know the score.'

She looked at his ruggedly handsome face and she could easily imagine the countless affairs he must have had. There couldn't be a woman alive who could possibly resist his charms and as inexperienced as she was, which he had easily recognised, she knew she had been made love to by an expert!

'So you know the score?' He repeated her words,

making them sound utterly foolish and incredibly naïve. 'And just what is the score?'

She shifted uncomfortably, clutching at the towel he had wrapped around her and was still wearing. 'Well for one thing I certainly wouldn't expect you to marry me just because,' she swallowed hard, 'just because we made love a few times. After all, everyone does it nowadays. It's just a fact of life.' Anger crept into her voice. 'Who do you think you are anyway? You're making it sound as though I've practically begged on my knees for you to make love to me. You're not the only man around, although to listen you, you must think you are!'

He was watching her as she spoke and Eden became aware of a curious sensation in the pit of her stomach as her heart flipped crazily in her chest. Without warning he walked over to her and snatched the towel from her trembling body. The soft swells of her breasts were gently heaving above the band of her bathing suit and the tanned skin of her slight shoulders shone smoothly under the ceiling light. His eyes swept over her, from the top of her newly styled haircut down to the slender curves of her ankles.

A cynical smile curved his lips and cruelty entered his eyes. 'So the little maiden has been completely aroused and her basic instincts cry out for more! Well, my little rose-bud, gather your things and move into my bedroom. I'll do what I can to make you blossom!'

She glared up at him, hating him. 'Why you pompous, arrogant swine! I would prefer to be a shrivelled, old maid rather than have the likes of you touch me. Oh, yes,' she added quickly, knowing too well what he was about to say, 'you kissed me once but I had to suffer your abuse afterwards. I must have been out of my mind to give you the impression that I wanted more of the same!'

And with that she whirled quickly and raced down the short hallway to her room, slamming the door behind her before falling on to her bed. She had never known such humiliation, such degradation. How could she have possibly thought she loved him? He was cruel, heartless and she had been a fool to fall for his charms. Charms? she asked bitterly. What charms? A snake charmer? Hah! That was more like it. True, he had been kind to her when she had needed it most and he had helped her in a way she knew she would be forever grateful for but ... but he had accepted her love and then tossed it in her face. No, that was wrong, He hadn't accepted her *love*, he had accepted her *body* and made love to *it*! And now not even her body was enough for him. He thought she was using it to trap him into marriage. But even this was to humiliate her further. She could easily picture what would happen if she took him up on his offer and moved into his room. He would make love to her when it suited him and then toss her aside when he was finished with her. He might even expect her to offer him a polite and grateful 'thank you'. God, how she hated him.

She should leave immediately of course. That would be the sensible thing to do. She certainly was strong enough and even Doc McKinley would find it hard to recognise her. But she had spent all her money on her new wardrobe and her pride wouldn't allow her to borrow money from Joshua to pay for her flight back to Melbourne. And to be truthful she didn't want to return to Melbourne with all its sad memories. She felt trapped and indeed she was. She would have to work at least another three weeks as Joshua's housekeeper before she had enough money to take her *somewhere*, *anywhere*, away from him and away from Melbourne.

There was a sharp rap on her door. She sat up quickly and ran her hands across her face. Silly fool that she was, she had been crying and over *him*! Thank goodness she had locked her door, otherwise he would be in here right now, gloating probably over the fact that he had made her cry and probably wasting no time in pointing out her foolishness.

'Yes, what is it?' she asked, her voice sounding suitably annoyed that she had been disturbed.

'Dinner is ready, come and eat,' was the curt reply.

Dinner! She had forgotten he had promised to prepare their evening meal. Her stomach felt queasy and she had no desire to eat. Besides, a quick glance in her mirror showed her blotchy and tear-stained face.

'I'm not hungry. Go ahead without me.'

He rattled the door-knob. 'If you're not out in two minutes I'll break this thing down and believe me the consequences won't be pleasant!'

'Oh, how you terrify me,' she snapped through the key-hole. 'I'll be out when I'm ready and not a second before.'

'Two minutes,' he repeated arrogantly and she heard his steady steps taking him back to the kitchen, not believing for an instant that she would dare defy him.

And she didn't! When she appeared in the kitchen he gazed curiously at her red-rimmed eyes but said nothing. She took her place on one of the bar stools and looked glumly at the shish-kebabs arranged neatly on her plate. They had been expertly and artistically prepared with mouth-watering chunks of beef, lamb, capsicum, pineapple and tomato. There was a bowl of salad and a hot, crusty loaf of bread spread with garlic butter and wrapped in a red and white checked tea towel resting in a small wicker basket. Their glasses were filled with red wine and in the centre of the table stood the chipped crystal vase and in this was a long stemmed yellow rose. He had obviously gone all out to please her and under normal circum-stances she would have been deeply touched. But these weren't normal circumstances and he was a fool if he thought she could be so easily appeased. He had insulted and hurt her and she wasn't a child who could forget and forgive if a lolly was popped into her mouth.

The meal was delicious and she longed to tell him but she ate with as little aplomb as she could muster, swallowing the succulent chunks of meat like they were tasteless lumps of oatmeal. He appeared not to notice, eating his meal with his usual good appetite and more than once he complimented his own cooking. Eden merely shrugged, offering no comment.

'You look tired,' he said when the last bit of food had been consumed and the bottle of wine had been emptied, Eden drinking more than her usual share. 'I'll do the clearing up. You go to bed.' He gave a suitable pause before devilishly adding. 'My bed, of course!'

Eden stood up, her face pale. 'This afternoon I thought I loved you. I was mistaken. I hate you!'

A lazy grin spread slowly across his handsome

features, amusement touching the green glints of
his long-lashed eyes. 'Sure you do,' he drawled,
rising slowly to his feet. A long finger reached out
to stroke her cheek, moving tantalisingly down to
her mouth, tracing the soft curve of trembling lips.
'Like a bee hates honey!'

She brushed his hand aside, frostily meeting his
mocking glance. 'Make fun of me if it pleases you
but just remember that any game you're intent on
playing, you play alone. From now on expect
nothing from me other than what you employed
me for. When I've saved enough money I'll be
leaving here and when I leave, I'll be leaving
behind all memories of *you*!'

His chuckle followed her out to the terrace and
she listened to the sounds coming from the kitchen
which told her he was busily clearing away the
dinner dishes. He was humming cheerfully and she
tried to block these happy sounds by concentrating
on the star-lit night. The ocean sparkled beyond,
the full moon spreading a blanket of gold across
the gently rolling waves. The white sandy beach,
bleached by the ever present sunny days, stretched
like a ribbon of finest silk against the darkened
shore line. She would miss this place. She had
found peace and happiness here and despite her
brave words, she had also found love.

But life had taught her nothing was forever and
no one knew this better than she. Her lessons had
been painful, delivered with cruel blows, but she
was a survivor. Leaving Joshua was just one more
hurdle but she would master that like she had
learned to accept fate intended her to spend the
rest of her life alone, lonely, without anyone to
love, or to love her.

She had changed into a light dress for dinner

but in spite of the warmth of the evening she felt chilled. The sound of the dishwasher came to her from the kitchen which meant Joshua had finished clearing up. He would be in the lounge now either reading or poring over notes for his book.

But he wasn't in the lounge. She could see his dark head bent over the breakfast bar. As she entered the kitchen area she froze when she saw what it was which held his attention. The sketches Bob Hastings had done of her and Sam and the scrub turkey.

'These are very good,' he remarked, without looking up at her. 'Did you do them or do you have a secret admirer?'

'No, I didn't sketch them,' she answered honestly, 'nor do I have a secret admirer.' She decided to treat the matter casually. 'Someone I ran into sketched them. They are good, aren't they? The fellow shows real talent.'

His green eyes sliced through her. 'Fellow? What fellow? Where did you run into him? Other than today you haven't been off this property.'

'What business is it of yours where I ran into him. I'm not a prisoner here so don't think you can treat me as one.'

'Don't be ridiculous,' he snarled, dropping the sketches and advancing towards her. 'All I want to know is where you ran into him. The scrub turkey has been sketched near the banksia brush. Was this fellow on *my* property?'

'Yes, dammit, he was. You make it sound like *your* property is sacred ground. God, but you're insufferable!'

His hand snaked out and caught her wrist. 'As far as I'm concerned this *is* sacred ground. My ground! I've had experience with trespassers before. They have no respect for other people's property nor, so it seems, do you.'

'Me?' she gasped. 'What have I done to it other than improve it. I've cleaned out all the weeds growing in your flower patch and I've worked my fingers to the bone digging up and making a vegetable patch. You've allowed the whole place to run to rack and ruin. You haven't even got a lawn. The place is wild.'

'Wild the way I like it, the way it was meant to be. I've never intended it to be anything other than what it is. Bush, clean natural bush.' His eyes raked across her face and his grip tightened on her arm. 'Now where is this fellow?'

He was hurting her and she half expected to hear the bones in her wrist snap. 'What do you plan to do to him?' she gasped, as his fingers dug into her soft flesh. 'Shoot him on the spot?'

His mouth twisted contemptuously as his eyes bored into hers. 'I might!' His hands moved roughly up to her shoulders, his fingers repeating the punishment they had to her wrists. 'How many times have you met this creep?' he snarled. 'I've wondered where it was you've been spending your afternoons.' He sucked in a ragged breath. 'So it's been him you've been meeting!' A cruel snicker passed his lips. 'No wonder you wanted to swim in the surf. He must be camped out at the lagoon.' His eyes shone with a malicious gleam. 'You were protecting him from me, knowing full well I would drive him off my property. Drive away your *lover*!'

With a strength she never knew she possessed she wrenched away from his cruel grip, surprising not only herself but him as well. She half expected him to grab her again but to her great relief he gripped the top of the bar stool, his knuckles white as his hands curled around the wood.

'I wasn't protecting him.' A coldness, both mental and physical was fast filling her, robbing her almost totally of any emotion whatsoever. 'He's an aspiring young artist and you only have to look at the sketch of the scrub turkey to see how greatly he cares for the bush and all it contains.' She took in a deep breath. 'Look at the sketching of Sam. Only an animal lover could draw a dog in such fine detail.'

He picked up both sketches, tossing away the scrub turkey, his eyes resting on the one of her and Sam but she knew it was herself which was holding his attention. The sketch did her justice, she knew this and it also made her appear rather provocative, perhaps even seductive. She wished now she had never accepted them.

'Joshua,' she said softly, going over to him and placing her hands on his waist, her arms gently stretching around his middle. He had put on a yellow shirt after their swim leaving it unbuttoned. Her fingers stroked the silky hairs veeing down to the band of his swimming trunks, her hot cheek pressed against the broad expanse of his back. 'I only met him the once. Sam and I came across him on one of our walks. He's probably gone by now. He's just a kid really, young and brash.' She was caressing him now, her fingers creeping inside his waistband. He stiffened, covering her hands with his own.

'Cut it out,' he growled. 'God, Eden, do you know what you're doing?' He swung around, facing her, green eyes locked to grey.

'Yes, I know what I'm doing,' she husked softly, knowing he was fully aroused. 'At least I'm honest about my feelings towards you. You want me every bit as much as I want you. You *need* me as much as I need you! You are jealous of that young man because he sketched me and because you think I might like him.' Her eyes held his as she continued. 'You only *pretended* to be upset because he was camped on your land but that wasn't it, was it? You were *jealous* because you *love* me! Admit it, Joshua, you love me. I don't know how or why it happened but we love each other!'

Suddenly she found herself in his arms, her lips parting wide to receive his passionate kisses, his tongue exploring the sweet yielding softness inside, hands moving possessively over her body as she arched towards him. His hands moulded her to him, thrusting her against his hardness. 'All I know is you drive me crazy,' he groaned against the sweet nape of her neck. 'And I want you to drive me crazy!'

Life for Eden and Joshua changed after that evening. They were never out of the other's sight. Glorious day followed glorious day. All work on Joshua's book came to a complete halt despite her gentle pleas for him to work and her offers to assist with the typing.

Together they had gone to the lagoon but the campers had gone leaving nothing disturbed much to Eden's relief. The lagoon became *their* place where Eden discovered the pleasures of swimming naked. She was proud of her body, of the way she had filled out, not because she was vain but because of the pleasure it gave Joshua. He became her whole world, her heart and mind dedicated only to him.

They never spoke of marriage or of the future or where their relationship would eventually lead them. They were caught up in something neither had prepared for and although Joshua never once said he loved her, Eden knew he must. After all, she continually told herself, actions speak louder than words and if this was true as she certainly believed it to be, then Joshua must love her as much as she loved him.

Mail arrived. Eden would pick up an envelope and say, 'This is from Doc McKinley,' and she would put it down unopened on the counter while Joshua would pick up another and say: 'This is from my publishers,' and he too would put the envelope down unopened. The outside world wasn't invited or wanted, or so they thought. There was no room for intruders.

They were eating breakfast one morning when the telephone rang. Joshua had an unlisted number which very few had access to and even then it was only to be used in case of emergencies.

It rang several times before he reluctantly got up to answer it, speaking roughly into the mouthpiece. Eden saw his mouth harden and angry glints appear in his eyes. She also knew even before he had hung up that their 'honeymoon' was over.

She was right. 'That was Clare,' he told her, sweeping an impatient hand through the unruly mob of his hair. 'She's on her way here.'

Eden had been chewing on a piece of toast liberally spread with butter and jam. Now it felt dry in her mouth and she had to take a gulp of tea before she choked on it.

'Clare?' she repeated weakly. 'You mean Clare . . . the one who decorated the bedroom? That Clare?' *The one you slept with?* Icy fingers of fear clutched at her heart. She knew only too well it was *that* Clare.

'Yes.' There was a curtness in his voice she had forgotten ever existed.

'When . . . when is she arriving?'

'Tonight! I'll meet her at the airport.'

That would be at Maroochydore where she had arrived and taken a coach to Glen Rose, an hour's drive.

'*Tonight?* So soon?' Eden pushed her plate away, her mind in a whirl. 'But why is she coming?'

'She was concerned she hadn't heard from me. She works for my publishers. That's how I came to know her. Apparently, they're also concerned. I should have sent in drafts of my manuscript. They're way overdue.'

Eden's eyes focused on the pile of unopened mail and she felt terribly guilty that she had been the cause for his publishers' concern. His writing was his work, his livelihood and she had kept him from it and now apparently he was to be raked over the coals.

'And your publishers are sending *her* to straighten *you* out?' Eden could hardly believe it. 'Is she an executive with them?'

Joshua was deep in thought and it was a while before he answered and even then he spoke in a vague manner. 'Yes. She's been with them a long time and she's kept me on the track before. I guess they feel she can do it again.' He looked at her. 'She knows her job.'

'You sound . . . you sound like you *admire* her.'

'I do,' he answered honestly, stabbing Eden's heart. 'You might say we understand each other. Clare is a real trouper and one of the best in the business.'

Eden rose stiffly and turned her back to him. He came up behind her and gently caressed her shoulders. 'Clare won't be here long,' he assured her. 'You have nothing to worry over.'

'You told me once she sleeps with you when she's here.'

He turned her around to face him, his hand cupping her chin, forcing her to meet his eyes. 'Clare will have her own room, you will have yours and I will have mine. She'll only be here a few days.' He smiled down at her. 'I can manage if you can.'

'I'm jealous of her already,' Eden sighed, trying hard to smile but failing dismally. 'I haven't even met the woman and I'm jealous of her.' She shrugged her small shoulders. 'I've never been jealous of anyone before but I am now and it's a horrible feeling. It makes me feel quite sick.'

Joshua chuckled and smoothed her sleek blonde hair from her cheeks. 'Now you know how *I* felt when I thought you were meeting that artist in the wood! But there's no need for you to be jealous. Clare and I are friends. Nothing more.'

Her hands crept up to his, fingers entwining around his long, lean ones. 'Is she beautiful?'

He shook his dark head, green eyes alight with amusement. 'Next to you she's downright ugly!'

'But she is your friend,' Eden persisted. 'More than a friend. You must have,' she swallowed hard, not daring to look up at him as she continued in a low voice, 'you must have loved her to have slept with her.'

'What a little innocent you are,' he gently mocked her. 'A man doesn't have to love a woman to sleep with her. It's enough if they're friends.'

'Is that what we are Joshua?' she dared to ask. 'Just ... friends?' Her heart stopped beating as she awaited his reply. How many times had she told him she loved him waiting for him to admit the same. But he never had. Not once. He kissed the tip of her nose.

'You know damned well how I feel about you,' he drawled and Eden sighed, knowing she had to be content with that. Perhaps he was incapable of saying, 'I love you' she continued to think. After all, what were words? Mere utterances, that was all.

'Now let's cut out this nonsense and start preparing for Clare,' he said, breaking into her worried thoughts. 'I'll drive into Noosa and pick up some supplies. Want to come?'

'No ... no,' she answered vaguely. 'You go. I ... I had better get started on the cabin.'

He laughed. 'That's right. I keep forgetting you're my housekeeper.'

Eden wasn't amused but his remark caused her thoughts to travel in another direction. 'That's another thing,' she said stiffly. 'How are you going to explain my presence?'

'What do you mean?'

'Clare. Naturally she will wonder *why* I'm here. What I'm *doing* here. I doubt she will believe I'm your housekeeper.'

'Clare will form her own opinions without any help from us. Now stop fretting.'

'She will think I'm your *mistress*! She will blame me for keeping you from your work. Your publishers ...'

His eyes hardened. 'My publishers don't own me, neither does Clare. You're the one who concerns me and if having Clare here is going to upset you then I shall book her into one of the resorts.'

That would be much, much better, Eden allowed herself the luxury of thinking. Aloud she said: 'But you can't do that! Not if it's here she's used to staying. Better buy me a great big apron in Noosa. I'll do my darndest to behave like a housekeeper straight out of domestic school!'

CHAPTER SEVEN

WHILE Joshua was off getting supplies at Noosa, Eden busied herself around the cabin. There was really very little to do but it kept her from thinking. When he came back she put away the groceries while he got ready to pick up Clare.

He came into the kitchen smiling and totally relaxed. If it was possible his eyes were even greener than when she first met him, his ultra-long lashes giving a mysterious aura to their depths. Despite what his publishers *and Clare* thought, he had needed this rest, all traces of harshness long gone from his handsome features. Now, dressed in white slacks and navy blue shirt, he appeared fresh and totally at ease. Eden couldn't help wondering if he wasn't looking forward to seeing Clare.

'Please come with me,' he asked again. 'It's a pleasant drive.'

Eden shook her head. 'No, it's better for you to go alone. It will give you and Clare a chance to . . . to catch up on things and . . . and you can warn her about me.'

'But if you came with me you could get to know Clare during the trip back. Be old friends by the time we get here.'

Surely he wasn't serious? Despite herself, Eden had to smile. Men! They really knew so little about women. How could she possibly become a friend of Clare's when Clare was coming here to stir things up, maybe even break things up between herself and Joshua. Joshua had said Clare was a

friend. But he had made love to her hadn't he?
Was Eden too merely a friend? Oh, if only he had
once, just once said he loved her then she wouldn't
be troubled by these horrible doubts.

'No,' she said wistfully, 'I really do think it best
if you went on your own. There are still a few
things I'd like to see to before she arrives.'

'I'll worry about you here on your own. Sure
you won't be scared?'

She managed a bright smile. 'Scared? With Sam
here? Don't be silly.' It was Clare who frightened
her but that was something she had to handle and
come to grips with by herself. Impulsively, she
reached up and pulled his face down, standing on
her toes to kiss him. His hands slid down her back
and then he was crushing her to him, knocking the
wind from her lungs. At that moment she
wondered if he wasn't a little concerned about
Clare as well and what that woman could and
might do to their relationship.

'I won't be gone long,' he assured her.

'Take your time,' she told him. 'Please drive
carefully.'

And then he was gone. Eden watched until the
tail lights of the old truck disappeared over the crest
of the hill before she finally went inside. The cabin
seemed unbearably empty without him. Perhaps
she should have gone she thought now as her heart
thumped uncomfortably in her chest. Perhaps it
hadn't been wise to allow Clare alone with Joshua
for the length of time it would take them to drive
from the airport to the cabin. Perhaps the old
feeling they must have had for one another would
be sparked off and kindle and grow during the trip
back! Perhaps they might discuss ways of getting
rid of *herself* so they could be alone without *her*

around! Perhaps . . . perhaps they might not come back and she would be left alone forever in the cabin, just her and Sam! Perhaps she had only *imagined* Joshua loved her; perhaps it had all been wishful thinking on her part and Joshua had only used her as a *substitute* until Clare returned! Perhaps . . .! She put her hands to her throbbing temples. 'Stop it!' she moaned aloud. 'Stop this nonsense! He loves *me*!'

She turned to Sam. 'Sam,' she said. 'You've met Clare. Tell me truthfully now. Do you think Joshua might, well, *care* for her?'

Eden stared miserably at Sam's answering frown. 'I see,' she murmured. 'That bad, eh? Well, I'll just have to wait and see how he handles her . . . *us*!' She stroked his regal head and couldn't help thinking how sad he looked, almost as if only he knew what was in store for all of them!

'Come on,' she murmured, turning away from those big, woeful eyes, 'I'll get your dinner.'

It had been arranged that she would have supper ready and waiting for when Joshua returned with Clare but Eden really felt she needed something now to try and get rid of the queasiness in her stomach. She made herself a light snack and ate it standing by the kitchen sink watching while Sam ate his own. For once Sam didn't gulp his food, picking at it daintily while she in turn picked at her own. She washed the few dishes instead of putting them in the dishwasher. Everything must be spotless for Clare.

Clare became a giant in her mind, a giant who could crush and destroy her unless she did everything perfectly. It didn't occur to Eden that because she had lost her family she had placed all her love and trust in Joshua. Now that love and

trust was once again threatened and her old
vulnerability returned with a vengeance.

She walked around the cabin plumping up
cushions and rearranging magazines. She did
everything over again from mopping the floors to
dusting the furniture. Imaginary smudges were
scrubbed from the fridge and the freezer. She
polished all the glasses and cutlery until they
sparkled and shone. The salad in the fridge was
checked several times and the dessert, a pavlova
rich with fresh fruit and thick swirls of cream, was
eyed critically. She groomed Sam, cleaned his nails
and checked his teeth for plaque. All the while her
eyes were on the clock. Finally she got ready
herself, showering and shampooing her hair
although she had washed it that morning. She
dressed and then decided her dress wasn't suitable.
It was a pale grey frock which heightened the grey
in her eyes and she knew she looked especially nice
in it with her golden tan and white streaks the sun
had bleached into her blonde hair.

But that was the trouble. She looked *too* nice!
What *should* she wear? She didn't believe for a
minute that Joshua would tell Clare she was his
housekeeper. Glory be, that had long become a joke
between them but on the other hand she didn't want
to give the impression that she was . . . that she was
what? His mistress? Shame for thinking such a thing!
What, then? A relative? Clare probably knew all his
relatives. His hostess? Eden brightened. Yes, of
course, his hostess. Then she frowned. A hostess
who *lived* here? Finally she dressed casually into a
pastel shade of green cotton slacks with a matching
green and white striped jersey top. She had settled
for 'friend'. If Joshua wanted to add to that then it
was up to him. In the meantime, Clare couldn't

possibly object to a mere friend sharing the cabin with Joshua now could she?

This should have made her feel better but it didn't. The minutes ticked by with agonising slowness. What were they talking about? Where *were* they? They should have been here ten minutes ago. Finally she heard the truck tearing down the long drive and she raced quickly around checking on everything yet again. When Joshua stepped through the kitchen door with Clare at his side Eden rose from one of the over-stuffed lounge chairs with a magazine in her hand looking for all the world like she had spent the time quietly reading!

While Joshua introduced them, each woman took an immediate dislike to the other. So this is Clare Morgan, Eden was thinking. Clare's hair was every bit as black as Joshua's only it was easy to see Clare's colour came from a bottle. Her hair was swept back from her face, severe, not a strand out of place. Her make-up was flawless, expertly applied. And she was tall, much taller than Eden and her thin black brows were arched arrogantly as she peered from her superior height down at Eden and Eden knew this look, this stance was to make her feel somehow inferior. She had run into this type of female before. One of the matrons she had trained under at the hospital had been the same, delighting in making young nurses squirm and feel utterly useless.

Eden smiled sweetly and extended her hand and there was nothing for Clare to do but to graciously accept it, both women murmuring polite words of greeting while Joshua beamed down on them obviously pleased with how well they had accepted each other. If only he knew!

Eden was fascinated with Clare's eyes. Blue chips of ice! Her rouged lips were curved into something resembling a sneer. Without a word being spoken Eden knew Clare disliked her presence here and that she fully intended to see that Joshua got rid of her. By the manner in which Clare clung to Joshua's arm it was obvious Clare considered Joshua to be her *own* private property!

Everything about Clare was immaculate. Her hair, her make-up, her beautifully manicured and polished fingernails and her outfit. A shimmering pale blue silk which brought out the much darker blue of her eyes and in flattering contrast to her jet black hair. Clare was stunning Eden had to admit and she fervently wished she hadn't changed her lovely grey dress for her slacks and top. She felt like a tomboy next to Clare's elegantly clad figure.

'I'll take your cases to your room, Clare,' Joshua was saying. 'Eden has prepared supper but I'm sure there's time for you to get settled before we eat.' He cast Eden an enquiring glance and she was quick to respond.

'Yes, plenty of time.' She followed them down the hall much to Clare's annoyance. 'This room, Joshua,' she said, opening the door to the room she had used and which Clare had used before her. 'I thought Clare would be more comfortable in here,' she explained. 'I've moved my things out.'

'You didn't need to do that,' Joshua drawled. 'Why give yourself extra work?'

'Oh, it was no extra work, really,' Eden told him, smiling up at him.

'Well!' Clare snapped. 'Had I realised I was going to be so much trouble I wouldn't have come.'

'Don't be ridiculous, Clare. You know we're happy to have you. It's just that Eden hasn't been well. I don't want her overdoing it.'

'And we certainly don't expect you to be any trouble!' Eden added with a smile but only Clare picked up the warning note in her voice and her blue eyes darkened with controlled fury.

'Jasmine!' Clare shrieked when she saw the bouquet of assorted flowers arranged in a vase on the night table.

Joshua and Eden turned to her, both surprised at her outburst. 'What's wrong?' Eden quickly asked, her nurse's training coming to the fore. 'Are you allergic to jasmine?'

'Yes!' Clare hissed, pressing a lace handkerchief to her nose and mouth. 'Get rid of it, Joshua, *please*,' she begged, her blue eyes as appealing as a child's as she peeped at him over the delicate lace.

Joshua grabbed the offending vase of flowers and held it behind his back. Eden could see he was greatly concerned and so, obviously, could Clare. She pressed her head against his chest while his free arm draped consolingly around her shoulders. 'Oh dear,' she sighed. 'I said I didn't want to be any trouble and now here I am causing a fuss.'

'Don't be silly,' Joshua crooned. 'It's not your fault you have an allergy.' He handed the vase to Eden. 'Get rid of these, please.'

Eden stared at them, dumbfounded. They were behaving as if she had deliberately planted the jasmine knowing Clare to be allergic to it. 'Yes, of course, but ... but what are you going to do, Clare? The jasmine is in full bloom. The property is swarming with it.'

'I've never known you to be allergic before, Clare,' Joshua put in, 'but if it gets too bad let me know. I have a friend at Noosa who specialises in allergies.'

Clare sniffed and nodded, pressing her head further into Joshua's chest. 'I'll be fine once Eden takes them away.'

'I think,' Eden said stiffly, feeling Clare was more allergic to herself than to the jasmine, 'the only real cure is to remove yourself from the source.'

Clare turned to glare at her. 'You mean fly back to Melbourne when I've only just arrived?' she asked incredulously. 'Sorry, but I won't be got rid of that quickly or easily.'

Joshua cast Eden a scathing glance. 'Now, Clare, I'm sure Eden wasn't implying any such thing. Were you, Eden!'

'No, of course not,' Eden replied, feeling she had been chastised. 'But if I were you Clare, I would wear a bandana across my face whenever I went outside.' She smiled sweetly at Clare's horrified look. 'A nuisance I know, but effective just the same. Well, I had better tend to our supper.' She smiled brightly. 'You must be starved.' With that Eden made a grateful exit from the room leaving Joshua to comfort the sniffing Clare.

Eden had prepared avocado soup, a delicacy for anyone coming from the colder southern states but here in sunny Queensland the fruit was in rich abundance and extremely cheap by southern standards. She was stirring the soup over a low flame when Joshua came up behind her, his huge hands circling her tiny waist. 'What a little vixen you are,' he murmured against her hair, 'hinting that Clare should go back to Melbourne and then suggesting she cover her face with a bandana!'

'I wasn't trying to be impertinent. I've seen allergies, worked with sufferers at the hospital.' She turned to face him, his hands moulding her hips to his. 'It's not a pretty sight.'

He smiled down at her. 'But you certainly are,' he growled, his eyes scanning her face as though he couldn't quite believe her beauty. 'It was good of you to hand your room over to Clare and the flowers were a thoughtful gesture.' He pressed her closer against him sending wild shivers up her spine. 'You must have been busy the whole time I was away. The place is shining.' He kissed the tip of her nose. 'What a little treasure you are.'

Eden slipped out of his arms, tying on her apron. 'That's what employers usually say about their housekeepers isn't it? That they're treasures?'

An easy grin lit up his tanned features. 'Now, none of that,' he warned giving her a light smack on the rear. 'Tease Clare if you must, but keep me out of your line of attack. Me friend, remember?'

Eden closed her eyes. *Friend!* So that's all he considered himself to be. *Her* friend! *Clare's* friend! God's gift to women!

'Do you think Clare really is allergic to jasmine?' she asked stiffly.

He shrugged his broad shoulders. 'I doubt it. I think she felt left out and was after some attention.' He sniffed appreciatively at the soup. 'Mmmm, smells and looks delicious. I'm famished.'

Eden was watching him, a small furrow between her brows. 'Clare will be wanting a lot of your attention, Joshua,' she said seriously. 'How are you going to manage *both* of us?'

His green eyes danced with devilish amusement. 'It won't be easy,' he sighed. 'What a terrible predicament for a man to be in! Two beautiful women and just one of me.' He brightened. 'I think I have a solution.'

'It had better be good.'

'It is.'

'Tell me then.'

He turned to the table where Eden had placed the salad. Popping a black olive into his mouth he said: 'Shifts.'

'What?'

He picked up another olive from the salad bowl. Eden pushed the bowl from his reach. 'Shifts,' he repeated. 'Which do you want? The day or night shift?'

Eden's face paled. 'You can't be serious?' she gasped.

'Of course not. I'm just trying to point out how ridiculous this whole thing is. We'll tell Clare we have a thing going. She's a big girl, she can handle it and we can all settle down and enjoy her visit.'

Eden felt sick to her stomach. Her hand fluttered to her throat. 'A *thing* going?' she asked weakly.

He smiled and nodded.

Eden's eyes widened in horror. 'Tell Clare I'm your . . . your *mistress*?' she gasped disbelievingly. 'That we're having a casual affair which she happened to interrupt? I can't believe you're actually saying these things to me, Joshua Saunders. Isn't anything *sacred* to you, anything at all? And what about Clare herself? I think she loves you, Joshua, I really do. She would try twice as hard to get your attention.' Anger filled her eyes. 'Or is that what you want? Do you want us fighting over you, the great and famous Gideon Shale, author and womaniser?'

They had been speaking in hushed tones but now Eden's voice rose sharply. 'I don't want anyone to know about us. I would be too ashamed!'

His eyes hardened. 'Ashamed?' he queried quietly. 'Of loving me?'

She hunched her small shoulders and looked miserably up at him. 'Not of loving you,' she husked, eyes shining with unshed tears. 'It's the most glorious thing that has ever happened to me, you know that, but . . .' She pleaded for his understanding, grey eyes clouded with misery. 'I don't want people pointing at me and saying there goes Eden Baines, Joshua Saunders' mistress!'

His green eyes hardened into angry slits. 'So what happens now, Eden? Do we rap our knuckles and call it a day? Do I beg you to forgive me for jeopardising your virtue? Do I look at you and want you but know I mustn't touch you because the eyes of society are watching and waiting to *point*?'

Eden swallowed hard but the lump in her throat refused to budge. She had given him every opportunity to confess his love . . .

'Yes,' she answered bravely, knowing she had to make a stand. 'Sooner or later our relationship had to end. I think I've realised it from the beginning but I was hoping . . .'

'You were hoping I would marry you!' he cut in savagely, and she was stung by the contempt in his voice. He grabbed her shoulders. 'Tell me, Eden, isn't that what you've been *hoping* for, *working* towards?'

The tears she had been holding back stung her eyes, glistening like tiny jewels on her silky lashes. 'Marry you?' she half sobbed, frantically wiping away her tears with trembling hands. 'Never! I could never marry a man with your conceit and arrogance.' She laughed shakily. 'I thought you must love me. What a fool I've been. You don't

love me, you never have! All along you've been
snickering up your sleeve thinking what a hopeless
little desperado I must be to actually be planning
on marrying you!'

The sharp click of Clare's heels could be heard
coming down the hall. Eden tore herself from
Joshua's cruel grip and turned frantically back to
the stove desperately trying to stem the flow of
tears streaming down her cheeks. She felt trapped.
Trapped because the man she loved was standing
behind her and she longed for him to take her in
his arms where they could both take back the
hurtful words they had flung at each other.
Trapped because Clare was now in the kitchen
making this an impossibility.

The soup was a blur in front of her as she
stirred, stirred away at it while Joshua greeted
Clare in a charmingly relaxed manner as if nothing
untoward had happened only seconds before.
Had her love meant so little that he wasn't in the
least affected that it had toppled with a few angry
words, a few home truths? But of course he wasn't
affected. He had Clare now and Eden no longer
mattered. He had probably planned this little
scenario in the kitchen, Eden thought as she stirred
blindly at the soup. And she had fallen neatly into
the trap. She was no longer his responsibility and
it had been her own words, oh, how could she
have said them? which had crushed what they
had.

Thank goodness Clare wasn't paying her any
attention at the stove. She was totally occupied by
Joshua who was complimenting her outfit and
fixing her a drink. Listening to his smoothly
timbred voice it was hard to believe that that same
pleasantly modulated voice had spoken so harshly

and so bitterly to herself only minutes ago. But at least he was keeping Clare occupied and that was a blessing. Several times Eden whipped up her apron to dab at her eyes and cheeks until all traces of her tears had completely been wiped away. It was only when she heard Joshua, followed by the gushing Clare leave the kitchen and go into the lounge area that she finally turned from the stove, the pot in her hands. She placed it on a thermal pad and then went down the hall to the bathroom where she planned to wash her face and cool her burning eyes.

But when she opened the door she stood staring in for several seconds, her eyes gaping with disbelief. Clare had obviously showered and had discarded several towels which were now lying in damp heaps on the floor. Dusting powder dulled the shining floor tiles making them slippery and unsafe to walk upon. Tissues, streaked with make-up, had been tossed carelessly towards the waste-bin but hadn't quite made it to the inside. Brown streaks of a liquid moisturiser had spilt from the wash basin and now rested on the floor. Lipsticks and other forms of make-up lined the vanity ledge, along with several perfumes, hairsprays and the like. It was obvious Clare considered the bathroom to be entirely hers and had no respect or consideration for others who must share it.

Eden picked up one of the damp towels and quickly wiped over the tiles before discarding it and the others into the wicker clothes hamper. The lovely green ferns in their colourful hanging baskets were wilted from the hot steam. Eden opened the windows to let in some cooling fresh air and to allow the almost nauseating mixture of several perfumes along with the hairsprays to

escape. She picked up the tissues and threw them
into the waste basket and then cleaned the sink. By
the time she had put the bathroom into its usual
good order and washed her own face and hands,
she found the soup had grown cold in the pot.

While she reheated it, she tried not to listen to
the conversation coming from the lounge area but
it was hard to ignore the bursts of laughter and the
general good humour of the terrible two as they
sat sipping their drinks while she tended to their
meal. Eden worked as slowly as she could,
dreading the moment when she would have to
announce the meal was ready. But there really
wasn't that much she had to do, having done most
of it earlier. The table had already been set, the
salad had been made, the soup was now hot and
the pavlova was resting in the fridge, alongside the
bottle of wine which would complement their
meal.

She was taking the hot crusty garlic bread from
the oven when suddenly Joshua was standing
beside her. His eyes skimmed quickly over her face
and she almost smiled when she realised he was
checking to see if she was still crying over him. The
cad!

'What's taking so long?' he growled, reaching
for the two foil-wrapped loaves in her hands and
turning them into the bread basket on the table.

'Everything is ready,' Eden answered smoothly.
'You and Clare were so obviously enjoying
yourselves that I thought it would be a shame to
disturb you when you were having such fun!'

He parted his lips to say something but then
immediately clamped his mouth shut. Whatever
the sharp retort, for she knew it would be sharp
and biting, Eden was never to know. Instead he

gave her a swift hard look and asked instead. 'Would you like a drink? Scotch? Gin?'

She had never seen him drink heavily although it had become their custom to share a bottle of wine most evenings at dinner. But now she realised he had already consumed several Scotches and although he was steady enough, his eyes were unnaturally bright. She looked at the glass he had carried into the kitchen and placed on the counter. Another double Scotch! If Clare had come all this way to help him meet the deadline set by his publishers she certainly had a strange way of going about it!

'No, thank you,' Eden answered stiffly. 'The dinner wine will be sufficient for me.'

'Prim little thing, aren't you? Little Miss Prim and Proper! She doesn't drink, she doesn't smoke and she doesn't believe in illicit affairs!'

'That's right,' Eden agreed, not wishing to enter into an argument with him in his present condition. 'That's what *I'm* like.' She watched sadly as he picked up the drink and took a long swallow from it. 'I'm not even a moralist,' she said, 'for if I were I would point out that you've had enough drink for one evening.'

His brows shot up in mock surprise. 'Don't tell me you're *concerned* about me?'

She turned away from him, pretending to check the table. 'Not *you* exactly,' she murmured. 'It was your liver I was thinking of!'

'My *liver*?' he rasped, his voice rising. 'Christ, woman, have you no feelings? What about my bloody heart if we must discuss anatomies.'

'I would worry about that too,' she responded in a warning tone. 'Alcohol is definitely not good for the heart!'

'Ah, but it soothes it,' he responded softly, eyes roaming over her body bringing fresh colour to her already flushed cheeks.

Clare came in, holding her glass. When she had come into the kitchen earlier Eden had kept her back turned and from her limited view from the kitchen area into the lounge had seen that Clare was wearing something red. The slinky red loungesuit emphasised every seductive curve of her body and her black hair was hanging loose across her shoulders giving a softness to her features which hadn't been there before. It was hard but Eden had to admit Clare was absolutely gorgeous. Clare's eyes were roaming suspiciously from Joshua to Eden and finally rested on Joshua.

'What's going on in here?' she demanded to know. Her eyes flicked briefly towards Eden. 'Surely you're not allowing this . . . this *creature* to speak back to you?' she asked incredulously. 'You did say she was your housekeeper, Joshua. *Really* . . .'

So, Eden thought. Joshua had told Clare she was just his housekeeper. Joshua had made her strong. She would show him just how strong she really was! Clare too. She squared her shoulders and raised her chin.

'Speak back to Joshua?' Eden shook her blonde head incredulously. 'I wouldn't dream of doing such a thing!' She smiled brightly at Clare. 'We were discussing the effects of alcohol. Now I for one believe wine served with meals aids the digestive system. Joshua, however, believes it has a soothing effect on the heart. What do you think, Clare?' she asked seriously.

Joshua was lounging against the breakfast bar, green eyes alight with amusement. Clare looked at him. 'Is she having me on?' she asked suspiciously.

He pushed himself away from the bar. 'I think she's having us both on. Eden can be utterly confusing at times. I know she has confounded me on a number of occasions.' His eyes caught Eden's, holding them in some mysterious look which made her forget all about Clare.

Clare broke the magic. Ignoring Eden, she spoke only to Joshua. 'Well I would watch myself with her if I were you, Joshua,' she rasped angrily. 'You've said she's been ill but she looks in perfect health to *me*! You also said she's a nurse. Doesn't it strike you as odd that she would prefer housekeeping work to her own profession?'

'I think she enjoys the peace and quiet around here,' he answered, carrying on the same theme as Clare, referring to Eden as 'she' quite as if Eden was in another part of the cabin instead of standing directly in front of them. 'She's a nature lover at heart . . . loves the bush and the surf and she likes taking Sam for long walks on the beach.'

'The stars,' Eden put in. 'Don't forget to mention that she also enjoys looking at the black sky filled with stars.' She turned serious eyes to Clare. 'You know what Melbourne can be like, all that smog. One hardly gets to see a star.'

Clare slammed her drink down on the counter. 'There's something going on here and I don't like the smell of it!'

'Smell?' Eden raced over to the stove. 'Good thing you mentioned "smell", Clare.' She tossed her a grateful smile. 'The soup was getting ready to burn!' Eden grabbed the oven gloves and lifted the pot from the stove. Joshua stepped quickly over to help her.

'You shouldn't be lifting heavy objects. Here let me do that.' And he took the pot from her hands

and placed it down on the counter. Eden gave
Clare a sheepish smile.

'Isn't he wonderful?' she cooed. 'Here I am . . .
his housekeeper, but he hardly allows me to do a
thing!' She looked up at Joshua and smiled
sweetly, ignoring his warning look that she was
going too far. 'Thank you, darling. I can manage
the rest.'

The meal was served and Eden waited on Clare
and Joshua with straight-faced dignity and all the
aplomb she could muster, ignoring the stony
silence of her two 'guests'. She chatted gaily
throughout the meal and before Clare had a
chance to offer help with clearing away one course
to make room for another (not that Eden
expected her to of course), Eden kindly told her
not to get up, that she could manage.

And manage she did. The meal was perfect. A
cordon-bleu chef couldn't have done better and
when Joshua complimented her, she allowed
herself to blush and murmur shyly, 'Oh, it was
nothing, really.' She longed to flutter her eyelashes
but decided that would be slightly over-doing
things. She mustn't overact her part.

That night Eden lay in her bed and listened to
the voices coming from the lounge. She had
cleared away the supper dishes declining help from
Joshua and now she remembered the hard look he
had given her before he and Clare had gone into
the lounge. She had bade them a cheery 'good
night' and retired to her cold, empty room,
looking solemnly at the bed she would sleep in
alone and remembering the nights she had nestled
in the warmth of Joshua's strong, loving arms.

Sleep was a long time in coming. Several times
the voices coming from the lounge were raised in

anger but finally all was quiet and the next thing Eden was aware of was the sunlight streaming across her bed. It was five o'clock and yesterday that would have meant sleeping in! Today she doubted she would have Joshua's company for a jog and swim. She slipped into her black bikini and covered it with a pink cotton top before stepping from her room to use the bathroom. Her nose crinkled at the stench of stale cigarettes. Even during the meal Clare had smoked between courses. The bathroom was a mess which didn't come as a surprise nor did the untidiness of the loungeroom. Glasses and several overflowing ashtrays littered the end tables and coffee table. Eden opened the patio doors and then went into Joshua's room.

He was lying on his stomach, arms flung across the bed. Against the white sheets his bare skin appeared almost black. His dark hair was tousled and the long, spikey lashes brushed against his skin. How she had loved to wake up and watch him sleep, her fingers lovingly stroking him awake . . .!

Now all she wanted to do was shake him roughly . . . which she did. 'Get up! It's well past five. I'll make you a cup of tea while you get ready.'

He rolled on to his back and opened his bloodshot eyes, evidence of the hard drinking of the night before.

'Your eyes look like Christmas,' she said. 'Green and red!'

He rolled back on to his stomach and groaned, 'Draw those blinds, will you,' and fell promptly back to sleep.

Eden opened the windows wider and drew the blinds. After tidying the lounge and the kitchen, placing the dirty glasses and ashtrays into the dishwasher, she fixed breakfast for herself and Sam. When it became evident that neither Joshua nor Clare were going to arise much before noon she set out on her jog with Sam running dutifully alongside her.

At the far end of the beach she was surprised to see Bob Hastings with a fishing rod slung over one shoulder with his morning 'catch' dangling from his hand.

'Hi!' Eden greeted him. 'I thought you had packed up and gone.'

'No, we ran into some other friends and we've pitched camp just over the rise there.' His eyes trailed over Eden's face. 'Gosh, it's good to see you again. I thought I never would. How are things?'

'Oh, all right.'

'You don't sound convincing,' he replied with a laugh. He held out his fish. 'Ever had fresh fish fried in butter over an open camp fire?'

Eden shook her head. 'No, never,' she confessed.

'Well, come along then and I'll introduce you to the gang and you can join us for brunch.'

Eden did just that!

CHAPTER EIGHT

'WHERE the hell have you been?' Joshua exploded when Eden returned to the cabin. 'It's well past four o'clock!'

'Is it?' His anger frightened her and even though she had prepared for it, expected it, she hadn't thought he would be quite so volatile about it. His eyes were fierce looking, appearing almost black as he towered above her, his hands clenched into fists.

'What do you mean, "is it"?' he mimicked her. 'You know damned well it is!' His eyes glared down at her and she tilted her chin defiantly, a gesture which only served to enrage him further. His hand snaked out and grabbed her hair, forcing her head back. 'Where have you been?' he asked, punctuating each word with a deadly cold deliverance.

'W-with f-friends,' she managed to stammer.

'With friends?' he snarled, making the words sound as unbelievable as if she had said she had gone to the moon and back. 'You haven't got any friends.' Understanding lit his eyes and Eden shivered. He tugged harder on her hair. 'Bob Hastings! You were with *him*?' The words were spat at her as a maniacal glint shone from his eyes. 'Who else were you with? What other "friends"?'

He released her hair and grabbed her shoulders, shaking her.

'Stop it,' she cried out, her voice trembling. Anger flared within her, giving her strength she never knew she possessed as adrenalin pumped through her veins. 'Take your hands off me!' she said as coldly as his own words had been delivered to her. 'You have no claims on me. I can do as I wish, go where I want to, have friends of my own choosing. And if you must know Bob and his gang invited me to move in with them, camp with them.'

'Oh, they did, did they?' He raised his hand to slap her but then dropped it to his side, his fingers clenching and unclenching as he fought to gain control of himself. 'And why didn't you? What held you back? You certainly were there long enough! Why? Was it so difficult to make up your mind?'

Hurt filled her eyes but she quickly lowered her lashes to conceal it from him. 'You have such a nice way of putting things,' she said at last.

He grabbed her and kissed her, his mouth punishing her with a savagery that was far more effective than the slap she had felt certain was coming. His mouth felt hard as steel on her own as he cruelly parted her lips, pillaging the soft interior, ravishing her until she could taste blood and knew it was her own. His hands moved roughly over her body, pinning her to him, hurting her until she finally gasped in pain. Only then did he release her but his face was still masked with fury. 'You're mine!' he told her vehemently. 'Mine! Just as surely as if I branded you!'

Her hand moved up to her swollen lips, a hand which was shaking with shock and humiliation. 'How *dare* you?' she flared, staring at him. 'You *hurt* me!'

'You're lucky I didn't kill you. That was small enough punishment for what I felt like doing to you!'

Her grey eyes were cold as steel as she glared up at him. 'You're nothing but an animal but please don't place me in the same category! You haven't branded *me*, Joshua Saunders, despite what that over-sized ego of yours might think. You've only succeeded in showing me your true colours. You fancy yourself as a prize stud and you see women as mere objects waiting to be serviced! I find you crude and objectionable!'

His lip curled. 'But not Bob Hastings!' The words were a statement and certainly not a question. 'Tell me about him. Where is he camped?'

'Not on your property nor anywhere near it if you're entertaining thoughts about driving him off. And yes, he is a gentleman and his friends are nice, charming people.'

'Hippies, no doubt! The inevitable drop-outs who fancy themselves as artists and poets and musicians.' He leaned against the breakfast bar, his eyes never leaving her face. 'So what did you do the whole day? Chant messages to the sun, spout poetry, smoke pot?'

He was quizzing her and she realised this, and she gained no small amount of satisfaction in knowing that she had ruffled his feathers. At the same time she was smart enough to know she mustn't antagonise him too far if she wanted to avoid his earlier punishment. 'I won't tell you if you're going to be sarcastic.' She went to the fridge and pulled out a pitcher of juice. 'Want some?' she asked and he shook his head. 'Where's Clare?' she tossed casually over her shoulder as she went to the cupboard to get a glass. 'Don't tell me she's still in bed?'

Eden was aware of his eyes still on her, watching

her every move. She filled the glass with juice and sipped it slowly, her fine brows arched inquisitively as she awaited his reply.

'She took the truck and drove into Noosa,' he replied at last. 'She grew tired of watching me pacing the floor like an expectant father waiting for your safe arrival. She wondered at my sanity when I took endless walks up and down the beach searching for you fearing you might have come to some harm or possibly drowned! She thought I had gone completely mad when I climbed one of the tallest melaleuca trees and searched for you with my binoculars! It was only the knowledge that you had Sam with you that kept me from tearing my hair out by the handfuls!'

'I'm sorry,' she said softly, going over to him. 'I truly am.' He was still leaning against the breakfast bar and made no attempt to touch her. She saw the anger in his eyes and also the concern and suddenly she felt extremely guilty that she had been the cause of it. She longed to touch him, to feel his arms around her, to tell him despite her earlier remarks that she loved him. But she sensed the breach between them, the breach which had started and grown wider with every minute since Clare's arrival. Thank goodness Clare would only be here another couple of days. They would patch up their differences after she had gone and probably even laugh about the whole matter.

'You still haven't told me what you did the whole day,' he reminded her curtly.

Eden sighed. 'Are you sure you want to know?'

'Every detail!'

She moved away from him. 'I ran into Bob at the far end of the beach. He had been fishing and had a marvellous catch. He and his friends were camped beyond the bluff and he invited me to meet them and join them for brunch.' Her eyes were shining as she looked across the kitchen at Joshua who was regarding her with a grim countenance which she ignored. 'Have you ever tasted freshly caught fish fried in butter over an open camp fire? Absolutely delicious!'

'So what else did you and Huckleberry Finn get up to after you ate the fish?' His voice was dark with mockery.

'Listen Joshua, I thought you were interested in knowing how I spent my day. If you insist on punctuating my every statement with your sarcastic quips then I won't continue,' she said firmly, standing her ground. 'After all I haven't asked how you spent your day with Clare!'

'I've already told you how I spent my day,' he reminded her grimly, 'and I'm fast losing patience in trying to learn how you spent yours!'

'Well, I wish I could tell you that we smoked pot and chanted to the sun and even went swimming in the nude because I know that's what you're expecting to hear,' she flared. 'But we didn't do any of those things although we did go for several swims, all of us decently dressed for the occasion.' They glared at each other from across the room and Eden felt the breach growing wider and wider. 'Apart from eating and swimming we didn't do much of anything,' she finished on a rather lame note.

'Now we're getting down to the nitty-gritty,' he confused her by saying. 'It's the *much of anything* that I'm interested in knowing about.'

Eden shrugged her shoulders impatiently. 'Clare was right! You are mad! You just can't believe that I had an innocent time with some innocent

people. You're behaving like a grizzly old bear
with a thorn in his paw. I'm sorry if you worried
about me but I can't understand all the fuss. I'm a
grown woman but you're behaving like I was some
sort of delinquent teenager on probation and that
you're my probationery officer.'

He ignored her outburst. '*Why* did they invite
you to move in with them? You must have done
something or said something which made them
feel you would fit in with their group.'

She squared her shoulders. 'I'll have you know
it was my friendliness, my outgoing personality,
my ability to accept others without condemnation
or judgment which made them want me.' She
laughed, albeit a little shakily. 'They certainly
wouldn't invite a surly character such as yourself
to join them!'

'Thank God for such small mercies!'

'Oh, what's the use of talking to you,' Eden
grumbled. 'I keep forgetting you're so much better
than we lesser creatures.' She peeped up at him
through her lashes. 'I heard you and Clare
quarrelling last night.'

When it became obvious that he had no
intention of telling her about it, she continued. 'So
that's how it stands. I'm given the third degree
about my activities but when it comes to you, your
lips are sealed. Oh, well, I didn't really want to
know about it anyway.' A pause. 'Did it have
something to do with your publishers?'

'We were discussing you as a matter of fact!'

Eden's eyes widened. 'You were? Why?'

'Clare can't understand why I keep you here,' he
answered coldly.

Eden hesitated. 'What ... what did you tell
her?'

'The truth of course.'

Eden felt faint. He had told Clare he loved her and she had rewarded him by staying away most of the day. How could she have done such a thing to the man she loved, to the man who loved her. Her heart was in her eyes as she said: 'You told Clare you love me.'

His eyes raked over her like cold green icicles. 'Like hell I did! I told her you were here for as long as it takes to get you better, then I would personally put you on a plane back to Melbourne.'

Eden stared at him. What a fool she was and how easily he could make her feel like one. 'Well if that's the truth why did you argue about it?' she lashed back, feeling her heart sinking to the pit of her stomach.

'Clare seemed to think you were well enough *now*.'

'And you don't?'

'I'm leaving that up to you,' was his cold rejoinder.

'Well, I'm glad Clare doesn't make *all* your decisions,' she answered bitterly. Her eyes felt like sandpaper had been scratched over them but she bravely fought back her tears. 'But Clare is right. I am better. You've done a marvellous job with healing my body and lifting my spirits!' She ran trembling hands down the front of her pink cotton top, avoiding his eyes. 'I'm ready to be taken to that plane but to avoid any inconvenience to you,' she added dismally, 'I'll leave when Clare does. You will be rid of us both in a couple of days!' Her cheeks paled as a horrible thought occurred to her. 'But perhaps it's only *me* you want to get rid of. You and Clare want to be alone! Now I can understand all that questioning about Bob and his

friends wanting me to camp with them. You were
hoping for a suitable home for me like I was a ...
a sick cat or something!'

'Don't be ridiculous,' he snarled, a flush
spreading across his face, making darker the deep
hue of his tanned face. He pushed himself away
from the breakfast bar and advanced towards her
and she could see the angry glints still gleaming
dangerously in his eyes. 'By your behaviour today
it would seem you *want* to get away.' He was
standing so close to her that she could feel his
breath fanning her cheeks. His very nearness
caused her pulses to race dangerously and her
heartbeats to quicken. She could feel his body
beckoning to hers and even though they weren't
touching it was like they were. 'Any more careless
behaviour on your part,' he warned, 'and so help
me God I'll thrash you. Don't *ever* leave this cabin
again without my knowledge.' He took a deep
breath. 'After all, while you remain under my roof
I am responsible for you.'

Eden knew she should let it rest at that. She
could see his anger was slowly subsiding but some
perverse reason, she didn't know what, made her
say: 'I went into your room this morning prepared
for our jog and swim. You as good as ordered me
out. I waited for you, fixed breakfast for Sam and
myself and tidied up after the mess you and Clare
had made. When it became obvious that neither of
you had any intention of seeing the light of day I
decided to go on my own. I didn't for one minute
think you expected me to sit and twiddle my
thumbs while you snored your head off.'

'You could have read a book. You didn't have
to go but you did.'

'Yes, dammit, I did! After the amount of

drinking you did last night I didn't think you would be in any mood for my company. Anyway, I thought I was doing you a favour. It was hard not making any noise and you know how Sam likes to bark at the parrots.' She shrugged helplessly. 'I never meant to upset you.'

'You've already said that but the fact remains you drove me half out of my mind worrying about you!'

'How many times must I apologise? What have I done that's really so bad? I don't want you angry with me . . . not with Clare here. It will only make things that much more difficult.'

The atmosphere seemed charged with electrical currents passing relentlessly between them. Neither moved but somehow their bodies were touching, the tips of Eden's breasts against his chest, his hard, lean thighs pressing against the yielding softness of her own. His dark head bent forward and she parted her lips to receive his kiss. 'Eden,' he groaned against her mouth, his lips nibbling at hers. His arms moved around her and she felt his fingers unclasping the top of her bikini. She shuddered in delight as his hands cupped her breasts. Her body ached with desire and she knew his did as well. Their bitter words were forgotten, the angry taunts history, as he pressed her closer to him while she returned his kisses with a passion which left them both gasping.

'Please,' she begged when she could stand it no longer. 'Please, Joshua.' There was no shame or embarrassment in her plea. Her love for him was all-consuming and there was no place for pride.

He groaned against the softness of her hair. 'Clare . . .'

Eden's head snapped back. *Clare!* She had

entirely forgotten about her. Reality returned with a rush and with it a strange kind of coldness which Joshua sensed. He tried to gather her closer but she held herself stiffly, a wooden object in his arms. His green eyes, still smouldering with passion, studied the smoky grey of hers. 'Clare!' Eden cried. 'How could we have forgotten Clare.' She struggled out of his arms and he let her, his arms hanging loosely by his sides.

'Clare must be fairly confident of you, leaving you here alone with me!' Her eyes were dulled by misery. All that had happened before, the hurtful words, the bitterness followed by their lovemaking, had taken their toll. Exhaustion swept over her, making her feel hollow and washed out inside.

He dragged a weary hand through his hair. 'I don't give a damn what Clare thinks. It's you I'm thinking of. You're the one who's worried about her opinion of us.'

Eden turned away from him, her shining blonde head bowed.

Sam's sudden barking made them both look up and they heard the roar of the truck as it skidded across the drive. Joshua cursed. 'She drives that thing like it's a battle tank,' he muttered and Eden watched as he went out to greet Clare. His black hair, rumpled from her hands as they had passed lovingly through every strand, rested against the collar of his red golf shirt in striking contrast. White shorts hugged the lean hardness of his hips and his long, muscular legs carried him in easy strides to the waiting Clare.

Eden fumbled with the clasp of her bikini top with stiffened fingers and managed to restore order to her hair by patting and pushing it into place before she too went out to greet Clare.

Joshua had opened the door of the truck and was helping Clare step down. Clare's arms went around his neck and she kissed him fully on the mouth just as Eden joined them. Clare's eyes swept swiftly and coldly over Eden's still slightly flushed cheeks.

Mistaking Eden's obvious misery and Joshua's stiff manner to mean a battle royal had been fought between the two, boosted Clare's morale. 'So you finally made it back,' she said to Eden. 'You certainly had a nerve neglecting your housekeeping duties for your own entertainment.' She turned to Joshua. 'I trust you fired her?'

Joshua regarded Clare with cold disdain. 'I did better than that!'

Clare looked momentarily puzzled but the apparent hostility between Joshua and Eden was enough to satisfy her.

'Good!' she said and Eden saw how she smacked her lips almost as if Joshua had put Eden on the racks. Well, in a way he had tortured her but not in a way Clare would have approved of!

Clare had done so much shopping that even Eden had to help carry in some of the parcels. 'I just *love* those little shops!' Clare enthused as the parcels were spread across every available space in the kitchen. 'They're all so *quaint*! And the shopkeepers are all so *nice*! They just can't do *enough* for you!' She turned to Joshua. 'Would you believe that most of them actually remembered me from the last time I was here? Look, I bought something for you.' And she scrambled through the various boxes and bags until she found what she was looking for. She held out a pink and mauve striped jersey and made Joshua turn around while she pressed it to his back checking the size. 'Just

perfect!' she squealed, with all the delight of a six
year old child.

The jersey was ultra-feminine and certainly not
the type of garment Joshua would wear. Eden put
her hand to her mouth to hide her smile while
Joshua shot her a murderous glare, daring her not
to laugh.

'I was thinking about getting you a little
something,' Clare said to Eden when all the bits
and pieces had been held up for inspection and
admiration and finally put away, 'but I thought
you would have gone.' The look in her eyes told
Eden quite plainly that Clare was speaking the
truth. Clare really did believe that Joshua would
have got rid of her.

'Oh, that's all right,' Eden murmured politely.
'But I really wouldn't expect you to spend either
your time or your money getting me something.
Besides, I went on a similar shopping spree not so
very long ago and have more than I need. But it's
nice to know you were thinking about me all the
same,' she added sweetly, her smile sugar-coated
which brought frosty glints to Clare's eyes.

Clare looked around the kitchen. 'I'm starved.'
She turned to Eden. 'Don't you think it's about
time you started preparing dinner?'

'Eden's had a long day,' Joshua put in. 'Unlike
us, she was up at her usual hour, five o'clock.
We'll go out for dinner.'

Clare was delighted. 'How wonderful! I'll wear
one of my new gowns. Where shall we go? This
really is an unexpected surprise. So unlike you,
Joshua. You usually have to be dragged to
restaurants.'

With Clare's departure it was like a tornado had
left the room. Eden and Joshua passed each other

amused glances. 'Are you going to wear your new shirt?' Eden asked him.

He shuddered. 'And be up for grabs by all the men?'

Eden laughed. 'Well, why not? The women all want you, why not the men?'

He stretched out his arms to her and she went willingly into them. He folded her close. 'Still love me?' he asked softly, his lips pressed against her hair.

She snuggled against him, revelling in the warm, protective embrace of his strong arms. 'I'll always love you, Joshua Saunders,' she whispered, tilting her face to look into his.

He smiled down at her, his hands cupping the sides of her cheeks. 'Even though you often say you hate me? Even though you find me crude and objectionable?' he gently taunted her, reminding her of her cruel barbs.

'Yes, even then.' She raised her hands and pressed them against his ears. 'Don't listen to me when I say things like that.' She took her hands away. 'Just listen when I say I love you.'

He grinned down at her, doing crazy things to her heart. 'Promise you will never go away from me?'

She nodded solemnly. 'Just so long as you promise not to put me on a plane!' And they both laughed, relieved that their quarrel was over and sharing equal responsibility for the start of it.

'But is it wise going out for dinner tonight?' Eden asked as she played with the strands of hair falling over his collar. 'I really don't mind doing the cooking and you could get some work done on your book.'

'I'm not in the mood for working,' he said. 'Besides, you deserve a treat now and then.'

There was a second shower in the laundry room. Joshua made use of that while the girls used the bathroom. However, by the time Clare had finished with the bathroom there was very little time left for Eden. Eden was standing patiently outside the door when Clare opened it, giving Eden a chance to survey the mess inside. Clare noticed her look of annoyance. 'Sorry about all that,' she said, waving airily at the scattered towels and other debris. 'But you are the housekeeper, dear, and I, after all, am the guest!'

'Being a guest in someone's home doesn't necessarily provide one with the licence to abuse it,' Eden returned smartly. 'I trust you've left me one dry towel?'

'Listen, little Miss High and Mighty,' Clare sneered. 'I've known Joshua for a long time. Long enough to know that he eats little girls like yourself for lunch.' Her eyes narrowed into ugly slits. 'I've noticed how you never take your eyes off him but don't be encouraged by any attention he might pass your way. He feels sorry for you, nothing else. In fact I get the impression that he actually pities you somehow. Now I wonder why that would be? What little sob stories have you conjured up to make him feel like that?' She laughed cruelly. 'Oh, well, it doesn't really concern me. Every female has her secret weapon. Yours is making men feel sorry for you. Mine? Well, that shall remain my little secret!'

'Clare?' Eden called when the other had crossed the hall to her bedroom. Clare turned impatiently.

'Well, what is it?' she snapped.

Eden walked over to her. 'Just *why* have you come here?'

A look of uncertainty passed over Clare's eyes. 'What do you mean?'

'You're not here to help Joshua with his book. You kept him up most of the night and you offered no resistance when he suggested going out tonight. I'd like to know what you're up to?'

'Would you, dearie? Well, isn't that strange because I would like to know exactly what *you're* up to!' And with that Clare slammed her door in Eden's face.

Eden sighed and went into the bathroom. Clare had certainly won that round she thought ruefully as she bent to pick up the towels. Between herself and Clare it would be a miracle if Joshua managed to get any work done on his book at all. Well, she would let him enjoy himself tonight but tomorrow she would put her foot down. She would insist that he work and she smiled at herself for her thoughts. Joshua would work when he damned well felt like it and nothing she nor Clare did could make him do otherwise.

Despite Clare's head start Eden was dressed and ready by the time Clare was and they entered the kitchen almost together, with Clare pushing slightly ahead. Joshua had just finished feeding Sam and he stood up from patting the dog, his eyes resting on Eden. She was wearing her grey dress, pink sandals and had a small pink shoulder bag draped over one shoulder. Her blonde hair fell in soft shining waves down her slender neck, framing the perfect oval of her face and highlighting the delicate features.

Clare was wearing an outrageous dress of burnt orange with slashes of red zigzagging throughout the swishy silk material. With her black hair and heavily made-up features, not to mention her height and outgoing personality, Eden felt slightly overwhelmed when she drew up alongside her. But

it was Eden who captured and held Joshua's
attention. He smiled at her, his eyes openly
appraising as his green gaze swept over her slender
figure and Eden felt a warm glow spread throughout
her body. He loves me, she thought happily.

Joshua was a picture of casual elegance. He had
on cream coloured trousers, an open-necked shirt
of the same colour and a lightweight jacket, the
colour of caramel, which was shades lighter than
the deep tan of his skin. He was in good spirits as
he greeted the girls, his dazzling smile spreading
over them as he put Sam out and then walked over
to the sink to wash his hands.

'Where are we going?' Clare asked. 'Did you
make reservations?'

'No need,' he drawled wickedly. 'I have an
understanding with most of the restaurants around
Noosa. I'm sure one of them will be able to
accommodate us.' He opened the door and bowed
them out. It was still light and the parrots were
chattering in the trees above clamouring for their
last bit of food before settling for the night. The
clear sky was losing its blueness taking on a pale
pink tinge. The air was sweet and clean and there
was a soft sea breeze. Everywhere there was the
sweet fragrance of jasmine but Clare appeared not
to notice nor did it seem to bother her. Eden
sighed from the sheer beauty of the closing day
and breathed deeply at the floating fragrances.

Joshua opened the door of the truck and Clare
quickly stepped ahead of Eden to be the one
sitting next to the driver. Joshua winked at Eden
while Clare was settling herself in the seat. His
hand swept down her shining blonde hair, his
fingers stroking the delicate skin of her neck,
sending wild shivers down her spine.

'Just wait here one second,' he said mysteriously and Eden watched while he strode over to one of the many frangipani trees and plucked off a velvety pink blossom. He returned to her and tucked it behind her ear and then stood back to survey the results. The sweet perfume of the blossom mingled with the other fragrances of the early dusky evening and brought a smile to the soft curves of her lips. She put up a slender hand to touch the petals. 'Thank you,' she said, as though he had placed gold, mountains of it, at her feet instead of a tiny flower behind her ear.

'It looks beautiful,' he said softly, adding, 'You're beautiful.'

During all this Clare was busily smoothing the skirts of her dress carefully under her. She looked across while Joshua was helping Eden into the truck. Grunting with annoyance Clare moved further over to give Eden the room she needed if the door was to close properly which meant, of course, that her skirts had to be rearranged.

'Why don't you get rid of this dreadful vehicle,' Clare snapped as soon as Joshua was behind the wheel. 'Or at least bring your Mercedes up from Brisbane.' She turned to Eden. 'Would you believe that he has the latest model Mercedes sitting idly in the garage of his Brisbane residence while he carts us around in this old contraption?'

'Harry puts it to good use while I'm not there,' Joshua answered smilingly, obviously used to Clare's criticisms.

'Harry!' Clare turned again to Eden. 'In case he hasn't told you Harry is his gardener. A dreadful, crusty old character. Fancy allowing your gardener to have full use of a Mercedes while you drive around in this thing.'

'But he likes taking Martha around in it,' Joshua put in innocently, and Eden smiled, knowing full well he was deliberately baiting Clare. Joshua had told Eden about his mansion overlooking the banks of the Brisbane river and about Harry and his wife Martha, both of whom had been with him for years and took excellent care of his property while he did his writing in the relative privacy of the cabin.

'I've long stopped trying to understand you, Joshua,' Clare continued, as they made their way along the winding roads towards Noosa. 'Other famous people enjoy the comforts of the fruits of their labour but you treat it all so . . . so casually!'

Joshua merely chuckled and the rest of the trip was spent in silence. The ocean had taken on a darker hue as the last rays of sunlight slowly faded from the sky, although it was still dusk when Joshua parked the truck in front of a huge triangular shaped restaurant, its walls completely covered in ivy, while wooden decks protruded over the roaring waves of the Pacific ocean. It was at once a most beautiful and quaint structure, while the decks lent a feeling of adventure and excitement as the waves crashed below. All around them, Noosa was coming to life. Fairy lights, strung from trees along the shore line, added to the gaiety and throngs of tourists, tanned and wearing clothing of every style and colour imaginable, crowded the streets and the sidewalk cafés.

Joshua led them up the steep steps leading to the restaurant and as he had promised, there was no trouble in getting them the best table in the house. It was too windy to dine on the decks but they were seated in front of one of the large picture windows.

As they sat down, the skies darkened above them.

'Oh, *look*!' Eden exclaimed, her voice hushed but vibrant with awe. The moon, a bright, gigantic orb of the most brilliant red appeared as if it was climbing slowly from the depths of the sea. It rose higher and higher until it was directly overhead, its colour slowly changing from red to orange. Eden felt as though she had witnessed a miracle and her eyes reflected that she had.

'Haven't you ever seen a full moon before?' Clare asked sarcastically.

'Not like that!' Eden answered. 'Never like that! It . . . it seemed to come from the water like some awesomely beautiful monster but of course I realise it was rising from the horizon.'

'That's why I wanted to come here tonight,' Joshua said. 'I knew it would be a full moon and I felt the same way when I first saw it. You can't get a better view of it than from here.'

Clare laughed. 'Really, to listen to the pair of you, you sound like children.' She reached for the menu they had been handed and flipped it open. 'Now let's get down to the business of eating, shall we, before you both start gaping at the stars. Honestly!'

Joshua caught Eden's eyes and they smiled. 'I guess Eden and I *are* a pair of romantics,' he said softly.

Clare's head shot up. 'Now what is that supposed to mean?' she asked sharply.

'Nothing you would understand,' he answered, but there was no unkindness to his tone. He was merely stating a fact which Clare didn't take offence to.

'Well, thank goodness one of us has her feet

firmly planted on the ground,' Clare said, her eyes returning to the menu. 'The garlic prawns sound nice. I think I'll start off with them.'

The meal went well, the food was superb and even though Clare monopolised the conversation, Eden didn't mind. It seemed Clare knew most of Joshua's friends here and in Brisbane and was even rather amusing with witty little anecdotes about this one or that. Joshua seemed to regard Clare with a fond sort of tolerance which Eden didn't mind under the circumstances. After all Clare was leaving tomorrow and she believed Joshua when he said he and Clare were only friends. So she chuckled gaily over Clare's witticisms and her heart hammered happily whenever Joshua gave her one of his special looks which were heavy with secret meanings.

The surprise came at the end of the meal. Clare announced it would be a lark to have a party. Warning bells clamoured in Eden's ears.

'When?' she heard herself asking weakly.

'How about a week Saturday?' Clare suggested to Joshua and Eden's heart stopped beating while she waited for Joshua to say no. To her horror he hesitated only a mere second before he nodded his agreement.

'Sounds great!' His eyes seemed to congratulate Clare on her brilliant suggestion. Clare shot Eden a triumphant glance while Eden realised too late that she had grossly underestimated Clare. Perhaps Joshua had too she thought miserably as Clare turned sultry blue eyes back to his.

Clare had managed to stretch her few days into an extended visit!

CHAPTER NINE

JOSHUA stretched out on the mat, his body damp from the surf, gleaming black hair flattened against his head. Eden was standing above him slowly rubbing her body with a fluffy yellow towel. They had jogged and had a swim in the ocean. His hand reached out and clasped her ankle, his fingers stroking the delicate bones.

'You're quiet this morning.' He smiled up at her. 'You were quiet on the drive back last night. What's wrong?'

'Nothing,' she answered on a sigh, sitting down beside him, her chin resting on her knees, solemn grey eyes looking towards the ocean.

He grinned and sat up, putting his arm around her bare shoulders. 'Nothing?' he queried, his hand moving slowly up and down her arm sending little shivers throughout her body. 'Come on, Eden, out with it. Tell me what's troubling you.'

She picked up a handful of the white powdery sand and watched as it sifted through her fingers. 'It's the party,' she answered, very much aware of his eyes on her.

He chuckled. 'The party? Is that all? The party isn't anything to worry about. Clare's an old master when it comes to that sort of thing. You'll see. She will take care of everything.'

She finally turned her head, eyes on his. 'You *knew* Clare would be here longer than a few days. The party is over a week away. I thought she would be leaving today or the very latest, tomorrow. Why didn't you tell me?'

He shrugged and fell back on to the mat. 'She told me yesterday that she's here on a working holiday. Poor kid. She hasn't had time off for months. I couldn't very well toss her out.'

'And the party? Did you know about that too?'

He rolled on to his side, arm bent at the elbow, his hand supporting his head. 'No, I didn't know about the party but it's a damned good idea. It will keep the two of you occupied while I get some work done on my book.'

'I see,' Eden answered stiffly, aware that he was becoming angry but then so was she. 'What happens *after* the party?'

'What do you mean?'

'You know perfectly well what I mean,' she snapped. 'Just how long will this working holiday last?' She rushed on. 'I can't share you with her, Joshua. I find her presence intolerable. She gets on my nerves! I'm sick to death of picking things up after her all the time. Besides, I know she doesn't like me here, she's suspicious of me. I can feel it. In fact I'm convinced that's why she's staying. She doesn't believe I'm your housekeeper, she as much as said so. She . . .'

Joshua pressed his fingers against her lips, silencing her. Amusement had replaced the anger in his eyes. 'You're over-reacting, Eden. I've known Clare for a long time. She's a career woman, definitely not the marrying kind, so if you think she's after me then you're dead wrong.'

'Women change,' Eden argued. 'Their careers might seem all-important at the beginning but then they start to realise something is missing in their lives. They long for a husband, a family, a home.'

She peeped sideways at him. 'And you must admit Joshua that you are a very good catch. You're rich and famous and handsome. I don't think Clare would turn you down if you asked her to marry you!'

He shuddered. 'As much as I like Clare she would be the last woman I would ask to marry. We would drive each other mad in a very short space of time. Besides,' he added, his green eyes taunting her, 'I'm not sure I'm the marrying kind. My lifestyle is too unpredictable. I enjoy my freedom and I guard it jealously.'

Eden stood up, her eyes reflecting her hurt. 'You should have said you guard it *selfishly!*'

He rose slowly to his feet, green eyes narrowed dangerously. 'We've been through this before. I thought we had an understanding.'

She shook her head. 'It wouldn't last and we both know it.' She bent and picked up her towel. 'Without total commitment there would be nothing solid to build our relationship on.' Her heart was breaking and she kept her eyes lowered so he wouldn't see the price she was paying to end their relationship. 'I'll stay for the party . . . to help with things . . . but then I'll go.' She looked up at him. A muscle alongside his jaw was working spasmodically. 'I'll never forget you, Joshua.' She swallowed hard. 'Never!'

She made her way down the beach, a lonely figure in a black bikini with a yellow towel draped around her shoulders. He watched her go but didn't follow. He kicked savagely at the mat stretched across the sand. 'Damn!'

Eden held back her tears as she walked down the beach. The time for tears was over. She realised she should never have moved in with him in the first place although she allowed herself the small concession that she really didn't have much say in the matter. But later ... later when she had become physically stronger, she should have gone. Her love for him had kept her there just like it was keeping her another week. Joshua had said Clare was a whizz at organising parties and no doubt the 'whizz kid' wouldn't need or appreciate her help. But she couldn't go. She had to have just one more week of being part of Joshua's life. One week to last her a lifetime!

Clare was still in bed by the time Eden returned from the beach, which meant she didn't have to clean the bathroom before she took her shower. Eden took her time dressing into a pair of red and white striped shorts with a matching top and brushed her hair until it shone. She tidied her room, made her bed and then went into the kitchen dreading having to face Joshua but at the same time longing for the mere sight of him.

But he wasn't in the kitchen nor was he in the loungeroom. His bedroom door was open the way he had left it before they had gone to the beach. A glance inside told her he wasn't there.

Clare came yawning and stretching into the lounge.

'Why are you snooping around in Joshua's bedroom?' she asked, eyeing Eden with suspicion.

'I wasn't snooping,' Eden answered. 'I was just wondering where he could be.'

'Well, presumably he's down at the beach.' Clare's eyes narrowed. 'Shouldn't you know that? After all, I understood that was *one* of the things you shared!'

'Yes, our morning jog and swim is one of our great enjoyments,' Eden answered airily, wondering just how much Clare had guessed about their relationship. Probably all of it, she thought dismally.

'Didn't you go with him this morning?' Clare asked casually but Eden knew she was probing with more than just a bit of idle curiosity.

'Yes, I did as a matter of fact,' Eden answered conversationally, 'but I came back early.'

'Why? What happened?'

Eden turned to her. 'What do you mean?'

Clare laughed. 'You must have had a fight, or if you prefer, a lovers' quarrel!' She laughed again. 'Otherwise you wouldn't be poking around looking for him like a little lost sheep and I know you wouldn't leave him there all on his own because you can't bear to be away from him for one second.'

Eden smiled. 'Can't I?' she answered coolly. 'Then how do you explain yesterday when I was away for most of the day?'

Clare turned her back on her and walked into the kitchen to find her packet of cigarettes. 'Don't play the little innocent with me, dearie,' she answered, whilst lighting a cigarette. 'You were playing one of those little games women have played for centuries. You wanted him to go rushing after you, prove to himself how deeply he cares for you.' The blue eyes narrowed as she watched Eden through a cloud of smoke. 'But it didn't work. He made no effort to look for you. I would laugh if it wasn't so sad! I can picture you hiding somewhere, counting the hours slipping by without your knight in shining armour coming to your rescue. Finally, you had to crawl out of your hole and come back.'

'I don't know why I should bother telling you this but I spent the day with friends. Joshua was furious when I got back but even that isn't any of your business. I should have told him where I was going or at least left him a note. I behaved very badly.'

'My, god, but you're a prude! *Behaved very badly*,' she mimicked Eden. 'You act and sound like a child! I don't know how Joshua can bear having you around.'

Eden turned away from her. When you loved someone as dearly as she loved Joshua it was easy to admit you had behaved badly if that behaviour had caused pain. And despite Clare's cruel taunts Eden knew Joshua had worried about her and that he had tried to find her. But she didn't say any of these things to Clare. Instead she said: 'I'll fix breakfast. What would you like?'

'Coffee and some toast.' She walked past Eden, her nose stuck in the air. 'I'll shower and dress first.'

Joshua returned, showered, dressed and sat down at his typewriter with barely a glance or a word to either Eden or Clare. Clare told Eden this was typical behaviour from an author but Eden knew otherwise. Joshua was losing his adoring housekeeper, his live-in mistress and he was sulking!

As the days passed Eden was glad to have the party to keep part of her mind occupied. Joshua's behaviour frightened her and she worried about him. He pounded viciously at his typewriter and she was amazed the keys didn't break off and fly across the room. He took all his meals at his desk, hardly touching the food. He sat at the desk day and night and most mornings Eden would find him asleep with his arms folded across the typewriter, his dark head resting uncomfortably upon them. She went for her usual jog and swim but he no longer joined her. In front of her very eyes he became a stranger, and the few times he did spare her a glance, she saw she had become a stranger to *him*. His eyes were dark holes in his head, his cheeks hollow.

Throughout all this, Clare made endless plans for the party, changing her menu as often as she changed her make-up. The guest list grew and grew until finally it became obvious that there was only one way to accommodate so many guests. They would have to settle for a barbecue. Towards the end of the week Clare asked Eden to join her for the ride to Noosa to purchase the necessary foods and drink. Eden hesitated. She didn't want to leave Joshua alone. It was unnatural for a man of Joshua's size to go so long without adequate food or exercise. She was terrified he was going through some sort of breakdown and that he might do something to harm himself. She had tried talking to him but he had refused to even look up, his hands pounding, always pounding at that damned typewriter, drowning out her words, her concern, her love.

'I'm worried about Joshua,' Eden told Clare. 'I don't think he should be left alone.'

Clare stared at her. 'Don't be ridiculous,' she snapped. 'Besides I can't possibly manage all the shopping on my own. You've got to come.'

They were standing in the kitchen area and they could see Joshua at his desk, his head bent over the typewriter. His shoulders were hunched, his black hair in wild disarray and his face was drawn and haggard. It was easy to see he was on the brink of total exhaustion.

Eden shook her head. 'I can't leave him.'

Clare gave a low, cruel laugh. 'He's a writer. All writers drive themselves. He's doing well. He's pounding out one heck of a book. You should be feeling glad for him. He's had a rest and now he's working. Left up to you, he wouldn't get any work done at all.'

'But he's been at it day and night. You can see for yourself what it's doing to him. I admit I know very little about authors but surely they take an occasional break. He hasn't eaten . . .'

'Cut the act will you,' Clare broke in sarcastically. 'Think of the money his book will bring in. When I take those drafts back to Melbourne I'll probably receive a handsome bonus. After all, until I arrived here he had done next to nothing. I've always been a source of inspiration to him,' she continued dramatically, examining her long tapered finger nails. 'That's why I've planned this party. The party will be his little reward. You'll see, he'll brush away his fatigue and be the life and soul of the whole affair. I've seen him in action,' she continued, adding pointedly, 'you haven't!'

Eden took a long look at Clare. 'You're hard as nails,' she said at last. 'You don't care one little bit for Joshua. It's his money you're concerned with and the party is for you, not for him. If you had any compassion whatsoever you would call the whole thing off. He's not up to it. Surely you can see that for yourself.'

But even as she spoke Eden could see she was wasting her time. Clare was checking through her grocery list and if she heard any of what Eden said it had no effect on her whatsoever. She looked up from her list. 'Well are you coming?' She didn't give Eden a chance to answer before she added: 'Or must I disturb Joshua to tell him you refuse to help.'

In Joshua's present state Eden knew the last thing he needed was conflict between herself and Clare. 'All right,' she agreed reluctantly casting Joshua a final worried glance before she followed Clare out the door. Sam was snoozing in the early morning sun. Eden knelt beside him. 'Go sit with Joshua,' she commanded in gentle tones. Sam opened his eyes, immediately alert. 'Go sit with Joshua,' she said again, patting his regal head. 'Sit and stay with Joshua.'

Sam got up and walked through the opened door and Eden waited until she saw him stretch in front of the desk, head between his paws, brown eyes fastened on his master's face, before she turned and joined Clare in the truck.

'What part of Melbourne do you come from?' Clare asked, quite as if they were chums.

Eden named the suburb and immediately a picture of her family home sprang in front of her eyes. The beautifully kept gardens, the tree lined street, the Cape Cod structure, the back garden pool and the emptiness, the terrible emptiness settled over her in a shadow of gloom. It was no longer a home. It was a house. People made a home and there were no people living in her house.

Clare's eyebrows rose sharply and she looked at Eden with new respect. 'You live *there*? Your family must be loaded. What does your father do?'

Eden sighed. She knew sooner or later Clare would get around to questioning her about her background. 'He ... was in medicine,' she answered softly.

Clare didn't pick up the past tense. Instead she mentioned the suburb she lived in and for once Eden was grateful for Clare's self-centredness. Her favourite topic was herself and she went into long and boring detail about the little terrace house she had purchased close to the city centre and which she had poured *thousands* into renovating, and where she gave the most *divine* parties and had the most *interesting* neighbours and how *surprised* she was that *Joshua* hadn't told her about how he had helped her with the wallpapering of her attic *bedroom* which had the most *glorious* views of the city lights!

Clare went on and on while Eden stared straight ahead sadly wondering if she would ever be able to tell people about her family and the fact they were dead. She felt torn up inside. She had loved her family and she loved Joshua but there was no one to love her in return. Self-pity welled inside her and it was only Clare's presence which prevented her from crying. There would be no need to say goodbye to Joshua when she left after the party. They had said their goodbyes on the beach and he would be relieved when she was gone. She dared not think of the future and what life would be like without him. In a way she had Clare to thank, for if Clare hadn't arrived, goodness knows how long Eden would have remained, grateful for any crumb he might have given her.

Eden concentrated on the scenery unfolding around her. The poinciana trees were blossoming and their bright orange flowers against the blue surf splashing on to white beaches soothed her and by the time they arrived at Noosa's shopping district she had regained her composure if not her spirits.

Clare's great love was spending money. Joshua's money! They went only to the most expensive speciality shops where Clare charged everything to Joshua's accounts, no questions asked. It was

obvious Clare had done this sort of thing many
times before. From caviar to Bundaberg's famous
rum, from the finest cheeses and the best pâtés to
the choicest cuts of meat and the most exotic
fruits, Clare bought it all. As Clare had stated
earlier, the shopkeepers knew and treated her well.
And why wouldn't they Eden thought ruefully as
she saw the size of the amounts Clare signed her
name against.

It was late afternoon by the time they had
finished and the back of the truck was filled to
capacity. 'Oh, wipe that look from your face!'
Clare snapped, as Eden looked disapprovingly at
the wealth of food the vehicle contained. She had
stopped keeping a mental count of the expenditure
when the amount had climbed well into the
hundreds!

'The look on my face will be nothing compared
to Joshua's when he hears how much money you
spent!' Eden declared.

'And you're going to tell him I suppose?'

Eden stared at her, dumbfounded. 'Surely he
has a right to know! I wouldn't blame him if he
made you take half of this stuff back. But don't
worry, I won't need to tell him. Everything has
been neatly tabulated on his accounts. However, I
presumed you would have the decency to at least
inform him how much this party is costing him.'

Clare laughed. 'I've thrown parties for Joshua
many times. He likes things done in a grand way
and he's not mean when it comes to spending a bit
of money.'

'*A bit?* You spent a small fortune today.'

'A fortune to you maybe but not to Joshua.
You'll see.'

They were about to get into the truck when Bob

Hastings and his gang suddenly surrounded them. 'Hey, Eden, didn't you hear us calling you?' Bob asked smilingly, his eyes openly admiring Eden in her off the shoulder mint green sun dress. Eden was aware of Clare standing beside her, of her eyes agape with curiosity at the rather unruly crowd which seemed on such friendly terms with Eden.

'Friends of yours?' Clare asked rather rudely, her thin brows arched in open disapproval.

'Yes, these are my friends,' Eden answered honestly, smiling at each and every one of them as she introduced them to Clare.

'Hope you didn't get into any trouble last week,' Bob was saying, 'when you were so late leaving us. We were hoping you would come back.'

Clare turned to Eden, her blue eyes openly sneering. 'Has Joshua met this . . . this *gang*?' she asked.

Eden shook her head. 'No, but . . .'

'Then why not invite them to the party tomorrow?' Clare poured her charm on to the unsuspecting 'gang'. 'We're having a barbecue tomorrow. We'd be delighted if you could make it.' Her eyes swept around them. 'All of you, of course.'

'Sounds great! Sure, we'll come! What time?' came the enthusiastic rejoinders.

'Five o'clock. Bring your swimming gear. We'll swim first, eat later.'

Bob looked at Eden, who had gone suddenly pale. 'Is this all right with you, Eden?' he asked. 'You don't look very happy about it.'

'Oh, that's just Eden's style,' Clare cut in, her face breaking into a slightly indulgent smile. 'She's just worried about the party but with some of her own friends there she'll feel more at home.' She put a sisterly arm around Eden's shoulders, making her skin crawl. 'Right, Eden?'

There was nothing for Eden to do but agree. 'Right,' she echoed.

When they arrived back at the cabin, Joshua had cleared his desk of all work and covered his typewriter. He had showered and shaved and looked surprisingly fresh as he came out to greet them and although he had lost some weight it didn't detract from his appearance. If anything, to Eden's hungry eyes as she feasted on him, he was more handsome than ever. Sam bounded after him going towards Eden and nuzzling his head against her legs. She smiled down at him and rewarded him by gently tickling behind his ears. 'So you got him up and moving eh, fellow?' she murmured softly so only Sam could hear. 'Good boy!'

Clare was full of chat, monopolising Joshua's attention but when he saw the bounty in the back of the ute his eyes widened in surprise. 'What did you do? Buy up Noosa?' he growled at Clare. 'How many people have you invited to this thing anyway?'

'The usual crowd,' Clare answered, aware that Joshua was angry and annoyed. 'But when we got to Noosa, Eden ran into some friends of hers and insisted that we invite them, so naturally I had to get more food and drink. There were at least a dozen of them but what could I do?' She pouted up at Joshua whose face had darkened with rage. 'Please don't be angry with *me*, darling.'

Eden stared at her. How could anyone tell such a blatant lie? Clare had invited the gang because she considered them louts and because of their youth she knew they would never fit in with hers and Joshua's friends, most of whom came from the 'Who's Who' pages of society. It had been an attempt to disgrace Eden in front of Joshua and now apparently Clare was also attempting to place the blame of the exorbitant amount of food and drink and the subsequent costs firmly on Eden's shoulders, using Eden's friends as the culprits or accomplices.

Joshua walked over to Eden, his green eyes bright with unconcealed fury. She buried her trembling fingers into Sam's luxurious coat. 'Your camping mates! You had the audacity to invite *them* to *my* home?'

'I . . . I . . .'

'Don't be such an old fuddy-duddy,' Clare cut in nervously, obviously fearful that Eden was about to admit the truth. 'It should be fun having them here.' She laughed shrilly. 'Eden said you haven't met them, well, I'm telling you darling, you're in for a treat! They're all so . . . so *primitive*! Most of the boys have beards and the girls . . .! No style at all. Dressed in rags and none of them wearing bras. They should prove amusing to our friends. You know what I mean . . . off-beat culture!'

Joshua's eyes seemed to rip Eden's face apart. She tried desperately to tear her eyes from his but she stared mesmerised back at him, grateful that he was too choked with anger to speak! Abruptly he turned and began unloading the truck, refusing the girls' offers of help. Eden and Clare put things away as he brought them into the kitchen. No one spoke. Eden and Clare didn't dare while Joshua was in his present mood. Eden's only consolation, if she could call it that, was knowing Clare's little bit of mischief had backfired, placing her in Joshua's line of attack as well as herself.

When the truck had been unpacked he called for Sam and left the cabin. From the lounge doors Eden could see him sitting on the beach staring out to sea. Sam sat beside him and it was as if they were both carved from stone. Neither moved, they just sat. When it grew dark they returned and Joshua went straight to his room without bidding either Clare or herself good night. Eden fed Sam and made herself some toast spread with Marmite. Clare announced she was going to retire early and went gloomily to her own room. Eden sighed and leaned back on the stool. With Joshua and Clare in such happy frames of mind it sure was going to be one heck of a party. Eden didn't allow herself to think about Joshua. She had wrung herself out worrying about him and after the party tomorrow she would be leaving and that would be that. She would never see him again and his behaviour this past week, not to mention today, had told her he would be glad to see the last of her. She was no longer welcome in his home and he didn't need words to tell her this. His attitude towards her had spelt it out loud and clear!

The following day Clare worked non-stop on the party with Eden doing all she could to help her. Clare had a talent with food and this became apparent as time wore on. Beautiful delicacies were created and decorated and handed to Eden to store in the fridge. Dips were prepared for the prawns and other seafoods, and salads rich in colour appeared as if by magic under Clare's capable hands. Eden was impressed and she wasted no time in telling her.

Clare shrugged the compliment off. 'I always do my best for Joshua. Besides, I'm used to this sort of thing. I've taken courses on preparing party

foods.' She looked up from the kiwi fruit she was
arranging on a pavlova. 'Surely you didn't think
my idea of a barbecue was a few sausages and a bit
of meat thrown on a grill?'

Eden sighed. It was next to impossible being
nice to Clare. 'Well, it is the usual practice.'

'For you, yes, and for those friends of yours I
would say definitely, but to people like Joshua and
myself and *our* friends, certainly not!'

Joshua was still in his surly mood and Eden was
glad he was occupied in the garden setting up
tables and umbrellas and getting the barbecue
ready. No hamburgers for this crowd. Juicy,
succulent fillets of steak an inch thick were waiting
to be put on the barbecue, along with salmon
steaks, ham steaks and thick pork chops. Eden
wondered how much food would be left over and
wasted. The prawns alone would feed an army.

Most of the guests were driving up from
Brisbane, an easy two hour drive, while others
were from around Peregian Beach and the Noosa
area. When Clare had put the finishing touches to
her fabulous creations, she left Eden to clean up
the mess while she made herself ready to greet the
first of the guests. The kitchen didn't look as bad
as it would have had Eden not cleaned up after
Clare the whole day. But there was still plenty to
do and what the dishwasher wouldn't hold, Eden
washed by hand. The first guests began arriving
just as Eden finished mopping up the floor. To her
horror, Joshua brought them into the kitchen, a
married couple with two young children in tow
who needed to use the bathroom rather urgently.
The introductions were brief out of necessity and
Eden volunteered to take the little ones, ushering
them out of the kitchen as quickly as she could,

aware of the picture she must make with her apron
still on and her hair tied back.

Clare had finished with the bathroom but the
children didn't mind the mess as they made use of the
facilities. After washing their hands and faces, Eden
took the two little girls back to the kitchen and
poured them each a tall glass of ice-cold fruit juice
and gave them some biscuits. The mother come in to
claim them and thanked Eden for her kindness.

In her room, Eden sat wearily on the edge of her
bed. She had a clear view of the back garden
where the guests were now arriving in droves.
Clare stood alongside of Joshua and Eden had to
admit what a striking couple they made. Both so
tall with a natural grace and elegance which none
of the other guests, despite their obvious wealth,
could hope to achieve. Clare was being the perfect
hostess and Joshua the perfect host. Just as Clare
had predicted he had shed his tiredness and was
being the life and soul of the party, his booming
laughter reaching to her room.

Eden sat for a long time watching them. Her
eyes followed their every move. She didn't miss a
thing. Not the way in which Joshua looked down
into Clare's adoring face, nor the number of times
Joshua put his arm around her waist or her
shoulders. Even their outfits seemed to complement
the other—Clare in her flowing lemon-yellow 'garden' dress and Joshua in his trim chocolate coloured
slacks and opened-neck shirt of the same colour.

Finally she got up to take a shower. She had
already put the bathro m in order, putting out
guest towels and the like so her shower and
shampoo was brief although she would dearly
have loved to stand for hours under the soothing
flow of water.

Back in her bedroom she quickly dressed having already decided what she would wear. A plain white sundress and a pair of white sandals. Nothing fancy but nice enough. She blow-dried her hair until it fell in soft waves across her shoulders. A bit of make-up on her eyes and a dash of lipstick and she was ready. Standing in front of the mirror she didn't realise what a picture she made. Her heart was too full of despair knowing this would be the last night she would see Joshua and that he would be spending it with Clare. Therefore, her natural beauty meant nothing to her. Not the smoothly tanned skin the colour of honey, not the sun-bleached shining hair, not the delicate bone structure nor the beautiful wide-set grey eyes with their silky fringe of golden lashes. Her feet felt like lead as she made her way to join the party. She was oblivious to the admiring glances from several men nor did she realise it was on account of herself that the punch table was suddenly surrounded by these same men all offering to pour her a drink. Joshua came up to stand beside her, a protective hand on the small of her back. She turned to face him but found she couldn't look into his eyes, focusing her attention instead on the top button of his shirt.

'Your friends have arrived,' he told her in a gruff sounding voice. 'Don't you think you should make them feel welcome?'

Eden followed his glance. She had completely forgotten about Bob and his gang. To her delight she saw that they had all dressed nicely for the occasion and had even started mingling with the guests who accepted them as equals and not as primitives from an 'off-beat' culture. Eden's eyes flew to Clare and she had to smile at Clare's look of disappointment.

'Which one is Bob Hastings?' Joshua growled beside her.

Eden searched for him amongst the crowd. Joshua had tightened his grip on her making her thrillingly aware of the power his touch had on her nervous system. 'There he is,' she answered quietly, 'the one with the blond beard.'

Joshua's mouth was set in a grim manner. 'Introduce us!'

Eden hesitated. 'Are you sure you want to meet him?'

He looked down at her. 'You bet I do!'

Eden introduced them and to her relief Joshua merely shook hands with Bob and welcomed him to the party. Eden was puzzled. She had felt certain Joshua would do something dreadful like order Bob and his crowd off his property. But Joshua had a smug look on his face and Eden realised Joshua felt Bob wasn't worth the effort. She smiled at his conceit.

After that the evening went well. Some of the guests went for a swim while others remained at the cabin eating and drinking. Bob and his mates had brought their guitars and soon everyone was singing and dancing. Eden was never without a partner but not once had she danced with Joshua, although she was certain he had danced with every other woman there. Most of the guests had departed when he finally claimed her for the last dance.

She went easily into his arms, her eyes closing when she felt them tighten around her. She drank in the scent of him and her own arms crept up to circle his neck. He drew her even closer, leading her into the darkest shadows of the garden. There he kissed her, hungrily, roughly, possessively and finally gently and she returned his kisses with the same hunger, the same need.

'*Joshua!*' Clare's voice brought them back to reality and Eden whirled to find Clare standing only inches away from them, her blue eyes glittering with hatred at Eden. Eden backed away but Joshua grabbed for her. In the sudden confusion Eden tripped and Joshua helped her to her feet. Clare's eyes continued to bore into her and Eden knew that Clare was about to release her fury. She tugged her hand from Joshua's and started for the cabin, limping because she had hurt her ankle in the fall.

'Now I know who you are!' Clare shrieked. 'I've thought from the beginning that I had seen you somewhere but I couldn't quite place you.' She paused. 'It was on television . . . on the news when you were released from hospital. You were limping then as you were just now.' She folded her arms across her chest, her lip curled in a sneer. 'For someone who managed to kill her whole family you certainly have got over it fast enough, dancing and singing and . . .'

'*Clare!*' Joshua snarled, taking a threatening step towards her.

Eden stared at them, her eyes two enormous holes in her white face. 'What do you mean?' she asked in a tragic little voice.

Clare smiled at her. 'Surely you remember, darling? *You were the one driving the car!*'

CHAPTER TEN

'No!' Eden screamed out as she raced along the beach. *'No! No! No!'*

Joshua caught up to her and she fought frantically to free herself from his grip. 'Let me go,' she pleaded desperately. 'I need to be alone . . . to *think*!'

'And that's exactly what you're going to do,' he agreed, picking her up in his arms, his dark head bent over her silky blonde one. 'But I'm going to help you!'

He carried her to the lagoon and set her down on the soft grasses beside the sand. His arms were around her, strong and reassuring as he gently rocked her to and fro. Overhead a thousand stars lit up the lagoon while the trickling waters helped to calm her tortured heart. He was giving her time to think and at last she spoke.

'I *wasn't* driving the car.' She looked up at him, her grey eyes pleading with him to believe her so that she could believe it herself. 'Dad would never have allowed me to drive his new car. He was still running it in. Mother hadn't even driven it yet, so why . . . so why would I be driving it? Clare's wrong. She was lying, Joshua. Do you hear? Clare was *lying*!'

He set her gently away from him so he could look squarely in her face and she in his. Her hands were locked firmly in his and she clung to them.

'Now I want you to remember everything about that evening,' he said softly, his eyes holding hers as he spoke.

Pain filled her eyes. 'But I've already told you what happened. Please, Joshua, don't make me do it again.'

His hands tightened around hers. 'You must! For your own sake, Eden, you must tell me again. You must start before the accident, the events leading up to it.'

She shook her head. 'I only remember what I've already told you ... the restaurant ... the celebration ...'

'But there's more than that, Eden. It's locked inside your brain and until it all comes out you'll never be a free woman. You've recovered physically ... I thought it would be enough but it isn't ... you're still quietly torturing yourself ...'

Eden stared at him. 'You *believe* Clare!' she gasped. 'You believe I was driving the car!'

'I *know* you were driving the car!' he stated firmly.

Eden felt herself go mushy inside. It was like every part of her had turned to soup. Joshua's face became two faces in front of her and then three faces. She felt him shaking her and then he slapped her.

'God, Eden,' he groaned, pulling her towards him. 'Don't do this to yourself ... to me ... to *us*!' His voice was ragged with emotion and when he released her, she was like a ghost in front of him.

'How could I have thought I loved you,' she whispered hoarsely. 'That you could believe such a thing of me. That ... that I killed my family!'

'You didn't *kill* them ... it was an *accident*, Eden. *An accident!*'

But she wasn't listening to him. It was like she had been turned into a marble statue, her beautiful face etched forever in pain. He touched her cheeks and they were cold. His huge brown hands cupped her face, his thumbs gently rubbing the frozen skin, his fingers stroking back the wispy tendrils of hair behind her ears. He drew her close to him, pressing her head against his chest, her ear next to his heart.

'So many times I've held you like this,' he whispered to her, 'when you were asleep and troubled by your dreams.'

His rapidly pounding heart stirred her, bringing life back to her soul. 'Is . . . is that how you knew?' she asked brokenly. 'Did I tell you in my sleep?'

He continued stroking her. 'No, you never told me.' He pressed his warm lips against her cold cheek. 'You haven't been able to tell yourself that yet, but I suspected and so I rang Dr McKinley and he told me.'

Eden stiffened in his arms. 'Doc McKinley told you? But he wouldn't do a thing like that! Spreading lies about me!'

'They're not lies,' he told her patiently but she heard the firmness in his voice. 'You've got nothing to be ashamed about, Eden. You can accept the fact that your father was driving but you certainly don't blame him for the accident because he was your father and fathers don't intentionally do anything to hurt their families. But you know your father wasn't driving and that you were. Children are vulnerable creatures and often hurt their families without meaning to and it's this which is torturing you. You hurt your family without meaning to. It was an accident!'

'I can't believe it,' she whispered brokenly. 'If it's true why can't I remember? I remember everything else.'

'Because you're afraid to but once you

remember then you'll no longer be tortured by nightmares and nagging doubts. Facing up to the truth is half the battle. After that the rest is easy.' He gathered her closer in his arms, reassuring her. 'Now I want you to remember and I'm here holding you, so there's nothing to fear.'

She put her arms around him as tightly as she could and he smiled down at her knowing she was no longer afraid.

'We were driving home. My sisters and I were sitting in the back and Mum and Dad were in the front. Dad was driving.' She looked up at him. 'See? I *wasn't* driving.'

'So what happened along the way? Did you stop somewhere?'

'No ... yes.' She frowned up at him, trying to remember. 'We ... stopped for petrol. Dad had an operation scheduled for the next morning and he wanted to get to the hospital early. I can remember everything clearly now, even what he said to Mum. He said, "I may as well fill up here and save time tomorrow."'

'Is that when you got behind the wheel?'

A roaring filled her ears and she pressed her hands against her throbbing temples. 'It ... I don't know ...' Her eyes were filled with anguish. 'Yes!'

Joshua held her face in his hands. 'Go on, Eden. Don't stop now.'

She spoke in a faraway voice. 'The girls and I got out to buy some candy bars and some magazines. We were about to get back into the car when my sisters started teasing Dad to let me drive the rest of the way. "It's only a few kilometres, Dad," they kept saying. "Let Eden have a go. Don't be such an old meanie." And so Dad handed me the keys. He . . .' she swallowed hard, 'he could never refuse us anything.'

There was a long silence before Eden could find the courage to continue. 'It was raining but I was driving slowly. Dad was sitting next to me and Mum had taken my place in the back.' She spoke rapidly now, anxious to reveal the truth not only to Joshua but to herself as well. 'We were singing silly little songs. There was a sharp curve coming up but I was well used to it. I slowed down even more when suddenly an articulated lorry came blazing around the bend. The driver had lost control and he was well over the dividing line, but I can remember I wasn't worried. I had everything under control. I can even remember manoeuvering the car and thinking we were safe . . . when . . . *when Dad grabbed the wheel, wrenching it out of my hands!*' Eden stared up at Joshua, tears streaming down her cheeks. 'The back of the car hit the lorry and we went crashing over the embankment.' She rose unsteadily to her feet, her face buried in her hands. He got up and stood behind her, his hands on her shoulders.

'If only Dad hadn't grabbed the wheel,' she sobbed, 'they would be alive!'

'If only you hadn't stopped for petrol,' he said quietly behind her. 'If only you had left the restaurant five minutes earlier or later. If only you hadn't gone out that night. If only the twins had been born a day before or a day later.' He took a deep breath. 'Can't you see, Eden? If onlys can go on forever but they don't solve a thing. Your father reacted normally. It was a natural reaction to grab the wheel. You were his daughter and he was trying to help you. You weren't at fault nor was your father. It was a tragic accident and you

needn't feel guilty about being the only survivor.
According to Dr McKinley you fought like blazes
to live.'

'But I didn't! I wanted to die!'

He shook his head. 'You showed courage that
night . . . a lorry coming towards you but you kept
your cool. You're a brave girl.' His smile warmed
her heart. 'Brave girls don't die easily.'

Eden took a deep breath. She felt calm and
peaceful inside. 'I must go home,' she said simply.
'I must go back to my home in Melbourne. I want
to see everything again. I want to see *them*!'

He understood what she meant. 'We'll go
together but not now. I've finished my book and
Clare can take it back with her. There's something
I want us to do before we go to Melbourne.'

'What's that?'

'Get married!'

She stared at him. 'You're joking!'

'I rarely joke,' he assured her quite firmly.

'And this isn't one of those rare times?'

'Nope!'

Eden searched his face but there was nothing
there to say he wasn't serious. She was completely
restored now and she owed her thanks to this
proud, arrogant man standing in front of her. She
loved him desperately, she would always love him
and because of this she knew what her answer
must be.

'I can't marry you, Joshua,' she said softly, a
faint tremor in her voice.

His black brows arched sharply as his eyes
widened in disbelief. 'Surely you don't mean that?'

She smiled at his arrogance, at his inability to
accept the fact that he had proposed and she had
turned him down. 'I do mean it, Joshua,' she

answered quietly, taking a deep breath. 'I love you too much to marry you.'

'Now what kind of insane answer is that?' he bellowed into the quiet night. 'Of course you love me! I love you! I've loved you from the beginning. That's why I went around to the resort the next morning to get you. I couldn't stop thinking about you. I kept telling myself it was pity I felt but I knew it went way beyond that. The way you have of looking at me, those eyes of yours!' He grabbed her close, his arms pinning her against him. 'If need be, I'll *force* you to marry me!'

She managed to squeeze her hands against his chest, to push back a little to see his face. His eyes were blazing with the love he felt for her but there was something else which caught and held her attention. She had never seen it in his eyes before; had never thought such a strong man would know such an emotion. But there it was, raw and naked and it caused a lump to form at the back of her throat. It was *fear* she saw! Fear that she wouldn't marry him.

Her hands were against his cheeks, smoothing away the taut grooves and her eyes shone into his until the fear went away. 'Joshua,' she whispered, her voice husky. 'I've never made it a secret that I love you. You will always be the only man in my heart, you know that but . . . but you value your freedom too dearly. You said it yourself that you're not the marrying kind and I don't think you are. You value your privacy. You would regard me as a nuisance after a while but you would be stuck with me and eventually you would grow to hate me. I couldn't bear that!' And she shivered just thinking about it.

He kissed her gently on the mouth. 'I could

never hate you, my darling.' He kissed her again. 'I admit I've said some pretty selfish things but I was going under so fast I was grabbing at straws.' She was kissing him now. 'This past week has been hell!' he went on between kisses. 'When you said you would leave after the party I tried to *work* you out of my mind. I didn't dare go to bed because I couldn't stand the thought of never feeling you close to me, not seeing your face last thing at night and first thing in the morning. When Clare said you invited Bob to the party I felt like killing you! I knew you weren't ready to go back to Melbourne so I assumed you were going to him. Even the thought of another man *looking* at you never mind *touching* you, drives me wild!'

'Shh.' Eden pressed a finger against his mouth. He was working himself into a rage. She smiled up at him, at the fiercely intent look in his incredibly green eyes. 'I was afraid you were going to cause a scene,' she said, 'but when I introduced you to him you didn't react at all.'

A devilish gleam shone from the depths of his eyes. 'Because I could tell you didn't care for him and because I had already decided it was me you were going to marry!' His eyes were filled with love as he gazed into her face. 'If you love me as much as you say you do, my darling, then please don't turn me down. I may not be perfect but my love for you is and I'll devote my entire life to making you believe it.'

They talked the rest of the night away and when the first pink of dawn shone down on them; when the bush canaries and the galahs and the cockatoos and the parrots circled around them and when the butterflies of every colour imaginable fluttered around them, Eden turned to Joshua and said: 'You said before that I was brave so I'll take a chance! Oh, yes, my darling, I'll marry you.'

He sighed and leaned back on his elbows. 'I wonder if other guys have had as much trouble as I've had in proposing to a girl. We're not even married and I'm completely exhausted!' He reached for her and pulled her down beside him and she snuggled into the warm circle of his arms. 'I wonder if I've done the right thing,' he mused, his fingers wandering through the silky tresses of her hair. 'Perhaps I've acted a trifle hastily. You're a bully and you might be mean to me. I'll probably have to serve you breakfast in bed each morning and wait on you hand and foot.'

Eden chuckled. 'Well, darling,' she said lovingly, 'you did promise to do all those things during your proposal. But don't worry, I don't want a slave, just you for my husband, perfect or not!' Her arms slipped around his neck and she added seriously, 'It took a completely unselfish person, a great man, to help me accept,' she paused and her smile was sad, 'what happened on that night. It will always be there but now I'm no longer haunted by their ghosts. I can smile and remember them as they were . . . as they will always be, as our family will be, happy and loving.'

The sun was high overhead and the green waters of the lagoon lapped peacefully against the white sands. The parrots, the galahs, the cockatoos and the bush canaries were nodding sleepily in the swaying branches of the casuarina trees. Joshua turned to Eden, his lips nuzzling the soft curve of her breast.

'We must go now, darling,' he said reluctantly. 'Clare will be wondering what's become of us and I told her last night, just after you ran off, that I would drive her to the airport this afternoon. If we wait any longer she will miss her plane.' His eyes gleamed down at her. 'And we don't want *that*!'

Eden sat up and rubbed her eyes. They had made love and afterwards she had fallen asleep in Joshua's arms. Now she looked up at him, a frown creasing the smooth line of her brow.

'Are you going to tell Clare about us?' she asked quietly. 'About us getting married?'

Joshua helped her to her feet and together they got dressed. 'Of course I am.'

Eden sighed. 'I wonder what she will say?'

When they returned to the cabin, Clare was standing in the kitchen, suitcases packed and by her feet. She took one look at Eden and Joshua. 'Don't tell me you have decided to get married?' she asked incredulously.

Joshua's arm was around Eden's shoulder and he hugged her to him. 'That we have and the sooner the better.' He smiled down at Eden's upturned face. 'Should we invite Clare to our wedding?' he asked devilishly.

Eden looked at Clare. 'If she would like to come?'

Clare looked at them both. 'Of course I'll come.'

Eden suddenly felt sorry for Clare. She realised at that moment that Clare had nothing. She went over to her. 'I'm glad, Clare,' she said honestly. 'Joshua and I would be hurt if you didn't.'

Clare put out a hand and touched Eden's arm. 'I'm sorry about what happened last night,' she said sincerely. 'I thought you knew ...' She held her head high. 'I'm not used to apologising but I know I hurt you and ... and I'm sorry.' She took a deep breath. 'Will you forgive me? For *everything*?'

Eden put her arms around her. Who knew about forgiveness better than she and who knew the destruction it caused if one wasn't forgiven. 'Yes, I forgive you, Clare,' she said simply and Clare knew she meant it and she sighed with relief.

Eden went with them to the airport. Clare had a final message for them. 'You're both wonderful people,' she admitted, 'but I know you, Joshua, only too well. I hate to say this but I doubt your marriage will last. I give you six months at the most!'

Eden and Joshua were floating in the lagoon. Between them, supported on either side, was Gideon. He was having a swimming lesson.

'I think that's enough for today, Joshua,' Eden said. 'He's getting tired.'

Joshua chuckled and swooped the baby out of the water and high over his head. Gideon roared with approval, six glistening teeth shining from his little mouth. 'And hungry too, I expect,' Joshua drawled.

Eden followed them from the water and watched while Joshua carefully placed the precious bundle on the mat beside Sam. Sam wagged his tail and nuzzled the tanned little body. Eden knelt down and tenderly dried Gideon, the bright fluffy blue towel attractive against the little boy's deep olive skin and unruly mop of jet-black hair. Long black lashes framed his startling green eyes which were alight with mischief. Joshua stood above them, his face beaming with pride and love as he gazed down at his little family. Eden looked up at him and their eyes locked and held. Both were smiling, each reflecting the other's love.

Eden's hair was much longer now, sun streaked

and blonde. Her love for Joshua and Gideon had brought her to full bloom and she was more beautiful than ever. Only joy and happiness lit her eyes, the haunted look gone forever. Joshua picked up Gideon, settling him in the crook of his arm while he reached for Eden's hand and drew her up alongside him, his arm closing around her slender shoulders. He kissed her and his hand slipped down to the little bulge barely showing in her tummy.

'Perhaps this one will look like you,' he said softly, his eyes sweeping adoringly across her face. 'A little girl with blonde hair and big, grey eyes.'

Gideon reached out and tugged at her hair. 'Mumma,' he said in his gruff little voice. He turned to Joshua and stuck a stubby finger into his eye. 'Dadda,' he announced before turning to look down at the dog. 'Samma,' he pointed.

'You little show-off,' Joshua chuckled, lifting the sturdy little body on to his shoulder. 'Say "Gideon".'

'Giddin,' Gideon answered promptly, clapping his hands.

Sam led the way and Eden remembered another time when she had followed Sam and where he had taken her. The cabin had undergone some changes. It was now much larger and included a nursery, a separate kitchen and lounge-room, a big family room and a formal dining room. There was a library filled with books, fairy tales and nursery rhymes alongside Joshua's political thrillers. There was also a den where Joshua could retreat and do his writing without interference, although this was a term Gideon had yet to learn!

They walked slowly, lingering along the way to pick some flowers and to watch the scrub turkeys running through the brush.

'Toikies!' Gideon announced, his green eyes wide with wonder as he became increasingly fascinated with his wonderful world.

Eden had made curtains to cover the many windows but these were rarely drawn and even then only at night. She sometimes wished her family could see her own wonderful family and there had been times when she would have dearly loved to discuss a few things with her parents but she felt somehow that they were with her and guiding her along the way.

She stopped short.

Joshua turned to her. 'What's the matter?'

'The door is open. I remember closing it before we went down to the lagoon.'

Clare appeared almost immediately in the open door. She had changed too. She had become matronly and there were streaks of grey in her dark hair which she no longer tinted. In Eden's eyes, she was far more attractive now than when she first met her. Clare reached out her arms and Joshua handed over Gideon.

'Now how's my boy,' she crooned softly, her blue eyes warming at the sight of her godchild. 'How's my big, big boy, then?' Gideon planted a big, juicy kiss on her cheek and Clare was delighted. 'Come see what Auntie Clare has brought you this time!' And off she went, Gideon tucked in her arms, his hands playing with her hair, messing it and tangling it, just the way Clare loved having him do it.

Eden looked at Joshua. Joshua looked at Eden. He shrugged his broad shoulders while she shrugged her slight ones. Neither knew why Clare was here.

'Clare?' Eden followed her into the hallway.

'Why didn't you let us know you were coming? We could have met you at the airport.'

'Nonsense,' Clare stated, her eyes hungrily devouring the sight of little Gideon. 'I wanted to surprise you.'

'Well, you've managed that all right,' Eden laughed, going over to sit next to Clare on the huge sofa. Joshua picked up the wrapping paper Gideon was throwing on the floor.

'Twuk!' Gideon exclaimed, immediately putting it into his mouth to chew on.

'Come here, Gid,' Joshua commanded the baby. 'Let's have a look at that.'

Gideon crawled over to his father, dragging the truck with him.

'Shouldn't he be walking by now?' Clare asked worriedly.

Eden laughed. 'Clare! He's only seven months old. Give the poor boy a chance!'

'I was walking when I was six months old,' Clare declared. 'And I was speaking in sentences! You're sure he's all right?' she asked anxiously.

'As right as rain,' Joshua said, as he examined the toy. 'I think we'll have to put this one away for a spell, Clare. It's got too many sharp edges. Besides, the box states it's meant for children between the ages of three and six.'

'Oh, dear,' Clare sighed. 'It looked like such fun.'

'Never mind,' Eden said, patting Clare's hand. 'He'll love it when he's older. You spend too much money on him anyway. We really wish you wouldn't. You're spoiling him.'

Clare looked fondly over at Gideon. He was sitting on his father's lap playing with the box the toy had come in. 'I've a right to spoil him,' she declared. 'After all, I am his godmother,' she said in a tone which explained it all. She looked hopefully at Eden. 'I suppose you'll be wanting me to be godmother to this second child?'

Eden glanced quickly over at Joshua and he caught her smile. 'We wouldn't have it any other way,' she told Clare and Clare leaned back in the sofa perfectly content.

'Now, about your third wedding anniversary,' Clare began.

Eden stared at her. 'Our third wedding anniversary! But Clare, that's almost a month away.' She held her breath. 'Is that why you're here?'

'Yes, I decided to come early to give you a hand.' She rummaged through her huge handbag. 'You've got enough to do with the baby and everything and now that you're expecting another, I thought it only right that you should leave the party up to me. I've drawn up the guest list and . . .'

Joshua grinned and held out his arm and Eden went over to share his lap with their son. Clare had become a sporadic visitor, not only here but at their home in Brisbane as well. They had adopted Clare into their family, knowing they were all she had. They never reminded her she had given their marriage only six months to last!

After all, Eden and Joshua knew it would last forever!

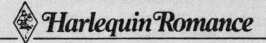
Harlequin Romance

Coming Next Month

2779   ONLY A WOMAN Bethany Campbell
A sports reporter's first assignment in Fayetteville,
Arkansas, brings her face-to-face with a basketball coach
whose game plan puts her job—and her heart—on the line.

2780   A FOOL TO SAY YES Sandra Clark
After accusing a therapist of giving his mother false hope of
walking again, a wealthy English landowner tries to involve
her in an affair. What kind of fool does he take her for?

2781   THE RIGHT TIME Maura McGiveny
It's painful to come across the right man when he belongs
to someone else—especially for a young woman who
rejected the same man six years ago when she followed
bad advice.

2782   THE PLUMED SERPENT Anabel Murray
Seeing him again brings back everything—the three days
they spent together in the jungles of Mexico, the danger,
the love and the heartache. What does he want with
her now?

2783   GAME OF HAZARD Kate Walker
An intruder at an isolated cottage on the Yorkshire moors
startles a British knitwear designer until she realizes the
man needs her help—and must accept her love.

2784   THE TIGER'S CAGE Margaret Way
Trapped! A young widow with her son feels cornered when
her husband's cousin hunts them down. Why won't he
leave her—and her memories—alone?

Available in August wherever paperback books are sold, or
through Harlequin Reader Service.

In the U.S.
P.O. Box 1397
Buffalo, N.Y.
14240-1397

In Canada
P.O. Box 2800, Postal Station A
5170 Yonge Street
Willowdale, Ontario M2N 6J3

Harlequin "Super Celebration"
SWEEPSTAKES

NEW PRIZES—NEW PRIZE FEATURES & CHOICES—MONTHLY

1. To enter the sweepstakes, follow the instructions outlined on the Center Insert Card. Alternate means of entry, NO PURCHASE NECESSARY, you may also enter by mailing your name, address and birthday on a plain 3" x 5" piece of paper to: In U.S.A.: Harlequin "Super Celebration" Sweepstakes, P.O. Box 1867, Buffalo, N.Y. 14240-1867. In Canada: Harlequin "Super Celebration" Sweepstakes, P.O. Box 2800, 5170 Yonge Street, Postal Station A, Willowdale, Ontario M2N 6J3.

2. Winners will be selected in random drawings from all entries received. All prizes will be awarded. These prizes are in addition to any free gifts which might be offered. Versions of this sweepstakes with different prizes may appear in other presentations by TorStar and their affiliates. The maximum value of the prizes offered is $8,000.00. Winners selected will receive the prize offered from their prize package.

3. The selection of winners will be conducted under the supervision of Marden-Kane, an independent judging organization. By entering the sweepstakes, each entrant accepts and agrees to be bound by these rules and the decision of the judges which shall be final and binding. Odds of winning are dependent upon the total number of entries received. Taxes, if any, are the sole responsibility of the winners. Prizes are not transferable. This sweepstakes is scheduled to appear in Retail Outlets of Harlequin Books during the period of June 1986 to December 1986. All entries must be received by January 31st, 1987. The drawing will take place on or about March 1st, 1987 at the offices of Marden-Kane, Lake Success, New York. For Quebec (Canada) residents, any litigation regarding the running of this sweepstakes and the awarding of prizes must be submitted to La Regie de Lotteries et Course du Quebec.

4. This presentation offers the prizes as illustrated on the Center Insert Card.

5. This offer is open to residents of the U.S., and Canada, 18 years or older, except employees of TorStar, its affiliates, subsidiaries, Marden-Kane and all other agencies and persons connected with conducting this sweepstakes. All Federal, State and local laws apply. Void where prohibited or restricted by law. Winners will be notified by mail and may be required to execute an affidavit of eligibility and release which must be returned within 14 days after notification. Winners consent to the use of their name, photograph and/or likeness for advertising and publicity in conjunction with this and similar promotions without additional compensation. One prize per family or household. Canadian winners will be required to answer a skill testing question.

6. For a list of our most recent prize winners, send a stamped, self-addressed envelope to: WINNERS LIST, c/o Marden-Kane, P.O. Box 525, Sayreville, NJ 08872.

No Lucky Number needed to win!

Explore love with Harlequin in the Middle Ages, the Renaissance, in the Regency, the Victorian and other eras.

Relive within these books the endless ages of romance, set against authentic historical backgrounds. Two new historical love stories published each month.

HIST-A-1